Chronicles Of a Single Woman

Relationships, Friendships, Hustle

By Tiffany Sharonda

This book is dedicated to God first because without him this would not be possible. I'm grateful for his wisdom and insight to writing this book. I also would like to thank my family and friends who supported me throughout this journey and motivated me along the way. You all know who you are.

Contents

Chapter One- Lurkin'

Sharonda

Sharonda walks in and sits down at the mirror as she applies her make up. She sticks to a very calm, natural tone to match her glistening brown skin. She heads over to the closet to find something to wear to work. "Ugh. This is so frustrating getting dressed for work should not be this difficult." Sharonda said as she continued to try on pants and skirts.

"No matter what I put on I still have a big ass." She ranted looking at her reflection in the mirror.

Sharonda settles for a cute pink pencil skirt with a tan silk dressy tank top and tan pumps with a pink bottom. She grabs her keys, purse and lunch then heads out the door. As she reaches the bottom floor, she walks outside to a cool summer morning.

She takes in the sun over her face and releases a deep sigh. "I can never get over how good it feels up here in these New York streets." Just then her phone rings. "Hello?"

"Hey beautiful." He said.

"Hi PJ?" Sharonda asked.

"What are you up to?" PJ asked.

"Headed to work duh." Sharonda rolled her eyes

"I have a real big head for you actually." He joked

"You are so nasty." She said.

He laughed. "I really am and you like it." He said.

Sharonda let out a deep sigh. "Anyways what's up with you?" She asked.

"I just got out of the shower about to get dressed for work but I called for my picture. You didn't send me a pic today." He said.

"I didn't take one. Plus we broke up you don't get those anymore." She replied.

"There you go with that again. I just want to see my "friend" then how about that?"

She laughed. "Ok sir well I'm almost at work. I'll talk to you later."

A man opened the door. "Oh I'm sorry I thought this was my uber." He smiled.

Sharonda thought, "damn he fine" as she began to exit the car. "It's empty. It's all yours." She smiled.

"Thank you." He watched her walk away. "Aye my guy can you wait right here for like 5 minutes?" He asked the uber driver.

The Uber driver nodded, "yeah she's fine as hell go head man." He said.

He ran up behind Sharonda and held the door open for her. "Let me get that for you." He smiled.

"Thank you." She smiled. "Are you stalking me?" She joked.

He laughed. "I promise I'm not but I wanted to introduce

myself and see if maybe we could at least go somewhere for lunch or dinner?" He asked.

She laughed. "Well first introduce yourself."

He blushed. "Oh I do apologize beautiful I am Matt and you are?"

"Sharonda. Nice to meet you Matt."

"Its nice to meet you as well Sharonda. Now can we get to that date?"

Sharonda's coworker walked up, "we're going to be late for our meeting honey hurry up." She stood blocking.

Sharonda smiled and rolled her eyes. She looked down at her watch, "meet me back here at 5pm."

Matt smiled and hugged her. "Definitely that works. Have a wonderful day beautiful."

Sharonda walks into the meeting room. "Good morning everyone," she greeted everyone.

The group responds, "Good morning. Hello"

"Are there any updates regarding the market investigation?" Sharonda asked.

"No there aren't. I spoke with them over the weekend and gave them another 48hrs." An employee said.

"Great that's awesome." She smiles.

Howie, the manager asked, "Sharonda may I speak with you please?"

Sharonda turned to him, "sure." She turned her attention back to the group, "you guys that'll be all, I am providing lunch for everyone today. You all have been working so hard and I want to make sure you know it doesn't go unnoticed." Sharonda said.

"Wow thanks so much Sharonda. You're an awesome boss!" The group replied.

"Yeah, she's right we want to make sure your hard work doesn't go unnoticed." Howie chimed in.

Sharonda smiles and thinks to herself, "duh I just said that" as she walked out the door with Howie she asked, "how can I help you?"

"Have a seat." Howie said.

"I have another meeting and I really want to make it on time." Sharonda stood by the door.

"I said have a seat. I'm your boss and I want to have a conversation." Howie said in a stern tone.

Sharonda cocked her head to the side, took a deep breath and sat down.

Howie sat at his desk. "What you're doing here is okay, but you don't have to do the extra stuff." He smiled.

"I'm sorry what extra stuff are you referring to?" Sharonda crossed her legs.

"No one needs food to do their job that's what they get paid for." Howie said.

"With all due respect to you I can careless about what you think I do for my employees. I have brought this company a lot and trained the best for this company. Remember you are NOT my boss yet. You're acting. You have a great day." Sharonda walked out.

Howie was hired only a couple months previously while they searched and interviewed for another manager. He clashed with everyone in management thus far because of his "I am better than you" attitude. He was a middle-aged white man who discriminated against Sharonda not just because she was black but because she was a woman. He did not like minorities at all and that was the majority of the staff.

The management team consisted of women and the employees were both men and women of various backgrounds. Howie had already stopped one employee from taking on "too many projects." But really it was because he was a Mexican who had more experience and more education than Howie and he wanted the manager position and would do anything to keep someone else from getting it.

Sharonda was lenient with her employee Amber who had 3 small children and was going through a really tough divorce. She would allow her to come into work at 830 instead of 8 like everyone else so she would have time enough to get her kids off to school. He stopped that, wrote her up for it and yelled and raised his voice during a meeting in front of everyone as if she was a dog just to prove a point that he was the main boss and everyone needed to be afraid of him. But that was the least of Sharonda's worries. Everyone wanted her to take the position but she was thinking of leaving the place as a whole.

As she headed into her other meeting, Sharonda scrolled in her phone until she found her group chat, "good sis."

Group text: If somebody doesn't get me off the plantation!!! –Sharonda

Group text: They up to it again over there girl? - Marie

Group text: Yes!! I'm so pissed!

Group text: Child you know I know. -Dajon

Group text: - I'ma need a drink or two or three tonight! - Sharonda

Group text: We got you boo. - Marie

Marie

"So this fashion show is big, so I need everything to be done and complete alright Londyn?" Marie asked

"Sis dang I got it don't worry." Londyn rolled her eyes.

"Alright I'm depending on you to make sure it's ready by tonight." Marie replied.

Marie was Sharonda's cousin from Georgia. They moved around the same time to New York. They were thick as thieves if you saw Sharonda you saw Marie and when you saw Marie you saw Sharonda. They are cousins but more like sisters. Sharonda was 29 and Marie was 30. She started her own business a few years after high school and while getting her degree she got her first shot at a really big fashion show featuring some well-known models. From there she moved to New York as her brand grew she thought she needed to expand.

Now living in a bigger market she was putting on her first big show in New York City where clothing execs are coming to view her pieces to offer on their online sites.

Marie headed out to New York's premiere Club Paradise where she's hosting the fashion show and the after party. They did a run through to make sure security was tight.

"I want all of their seats right here in the front. I want the drinks at the bar to keep going. I've put a lot into this one it must go right. No mistakes people." Marie said.

"Yes ma'am we got you Marie!" Alonzo who was djing the

event said.

"Thanks baby I know it's going to be fire!" She exclaimed

"Excuse me, Miss?" Security asked.

"Martin, Yes?" She answered.

"Ms. Martin, do you want everything at every door?" He asked.

"Yes I do and I think I sent over the logistics just incase I didn't I can email you right now." She scrolled through her phone.

Group text: Are ya'll on the way here? I am so nervous!- Marie

Group text: I am JUST getting off but I am finally on the way ladies- Sharonda

Group text: I just pulled up I'm walking in now girl.- Dajon

Marie is making sure everyone's outfits fit and everyone is in place.

Sharonda finally makes it in just before the show starts.

"Hi cousin!" Sharonda yelled.

"Fam! You made it!" Marie walked to Sharonda.

They hug and Sharonda gave her flowers.

"Aww thank you fam." Marie smelled the flowers.

"Of course boo you got this and I am soooo proud of you and Londyn!" Sharonda exclaimed.

"Yes, lil sis on vacay from school and she did a really great job helping her big sis." Marie smiled.

"Alright go out there and get it boo we are out there cheering for you!" They hugged and Sharonda went out to watch the show.

2 hours later the after party was going and Marie stood at the top as Sharonda and Dajon walked up to join her.

"Congratulations Marie!!! Your pieces were so gorgeous girl." Dajon said.

"Girrrl thank you!!" Marie danced.

"Fam! Bay-bae you did that!!" Sharonda walked up.

"Ya'll enjoy yourselves and I'm going to walk around and work the room a little and I'll come back up." Marie walked off.

Marie mingled and rubbed elbows with some big name brand companies.

"Hi Ms. Martin I have to say your fashion show was amazing." Ms. Sholow said.

"Thank you I'm so glad you enjoyed it." Marie smiled.

"I think we want to carry your brand in our store." Ms. Sholow smiled.

Marie's mouth widened with a huge smile as she shook Ms. Sholow's hand.

"Wow! I'm speechless." Marie responded.

"We'll be speaking with you soon and I'll have my assistant write up the papers." Ms. Sholow said.

"Okay great. Sounds perfect!" Marie covered her mouth.

Ms. Sholow exit the party and as Marie turned to walk back to VIP a guy gripped her arm.

"Let go of me." Marie jerked her arm.

"Damn baby why you got an attitude though?" The drunk guy asked.

"Listen you don't know me alright so go on about your business. You're drunk." She said.

"Fuck all that." He grabbed her and started to touch on her

Security stepped in and ripped him away from her.

The lead security guard yelled, "get him the fuck out of here!" He turned to Marie. "Are you alright Ms. Martin?" He asked.

"Yes I'm fine. Thank you." She smiled.

"No problem I would never let anything happen to that beautiful body or that gorgeous smile." He smiled.

Marie looked him up and down as he stood 6'5, all muscle and a thick build as she liked her men. "What was your name again?" she asked.

"Erick Williams." He replied.

"Thank you Erick." She smiled.

Sharonda and Dajon rushed to Marie.

"Fam you alright?" Sharonda asked.

"Yeah girl we couldn't get through the crowd quick enough." Dajon said.

"Yeah I'm good Erick took care of me." He smiled and walked away.

"Who is Erick?" Sharonda asked.

"Mr. Officer." Dajon smirked.

"Ahh, calm down he's just security." Marie threw up her hands.

"Mmhmm." Sharonda smirked.

"What?" Marie blushed.

"I ain't said nothing." Sharonda laughed.

Dajon and Marie both laughed.

Hours passed and Dajon started to yawn.

"Chile you so old." Marie said.

Dajon laughed. "That's true don't act like you about to be out all night though."

Sharonda laughed, "right."

"Well we are going to get ready to go. Plus my boo supposed to call me soon, ya'll know he out of town." Dajon stood.

Sharonda rolled her eyes, "girl bye. Alright fam, you good?" She asked.

"Girl I am good on cloud 9!" Marie exclaimed.

"Wait you got the deal?" Sharonda asked.

"Yes!! We got it!!" She screamed.

"Congratulations boo!!" Dajon said in excitement.

"Thank you!!" Marie jumped up and down.

"Yes!!! I'm soooo happy for you sis!!" Sharonda hugged Marie and Dajon followed suit.

"Excuse me, Sharonda?" A guy tapped her shoulder.

Dajon

Dajon and Marie both look to see who Sharonda is talking to. Just then her phone began to ring.

"I'm going to see ya'll later" Dajon hugged Marie and walked out of the club.

"Hello?" She answered her phone.

"What took you so long to answer the phone?" Derek her

boyfriend asked.

"I was saying goodbye to my friends Derek." She said.

"You see them all the time it shouldn't take that long to answer the phone!" He yelled.

"Derek calm down it's not that big of a damn deal." She said.

"Where are you?" He asked.

Dajon smacked her lips. "I told you I just left from being with my friends."

"What friends?" Derek asked.

"Derek do not start this you know who my friends are." Dajon rolled her eyes.

"Your ass needs to get home now!" Derek yelled.

"Why are you yelling? You are not my daddy." She said.

"Aight so you want to be a smart ass, ok." He said in anger.

Dajon got into an uber and hung up the phone. Derek tried calling back and she ignored the call.

She finally reached her home and hopped out of the car. As she was about to unlock her door Derek opened it.

"What the hell Derek?" Dajon jumped.

"You have not been with your friends dressed that damn sexy." He moved to the side.

Dajon walked in and threw her heels to the side. "How the hell did you get into my apt?" She asked.

"Why is your location off?" Derek questioned her.

Dajon continued to walk into the bedroom. "Derek you're making shit up. I'm going to bed."

"No the fuck you aren't." He grabbed her wrist and threw

her on the bed.

"Let me go!" Dajon yelled.

Derek sits on her legs and holds her down.

"What the fuck? Get up Derek!" She continued to yell.

"You went on a date didn't you?" He asked.

"No I didn't I was with my girls." She punched him.

"Ouch that hurt girl," he got up.

"Move out of my way." Dajon pushed him and went into the bathroom and locked the door. Derek banged on the door and she turned on the shower. Dajon cried until he stopped.

Derek waited until Dajon got out of the shower meanwhile he took her clothes and put them in the laundry. He fixed a bowl of her favorite ice cream and brought it to her.

"I'm sorry baby." Derek said.

Dajon turned the other way and continued to lotion up.

"Please forgive me. I just get so crazy about you baby and I apologize for acting that way. Will you please forgive me?" He asked.

Dajon continued to ignore him. Derek kissed her back.

Dajon moved her shoulder, "stop."

Derek climbed in bed behind her and wrapped his arm around Dajon and touched her spot instantly making her moist; simultaneously kissing her neck and licking down her back. He asked, "do you really want me to stop?"

Dajon shook her head no and removed her towel. Derek kissed her soft ass and continued to run his fingers around her love top. He bent her over and pulled her hair as his love entered hers.

They continued to make love through the night.

Chapter Two - Play Yo Part

Sharonda

Sharonda turned around to face the guy who tapped her shoulder. She remembered his face from earlier in the day. "Matt right?" Sharonda asked. "Yes that's right." He smiled.

"What are you doing here?" She asked.

"My mans invited me out tonight. You?" He asked.

"This is my cousin's party." Sharonda said.

"The fashion designer?" Matt asked.

"Yes she's dope, right?" Sharonda grinned.

"Yes she is congrats to her." Matt smiled.

"Thank you I'll tell her." She smiled.

"Yeah but I'm interested in you so let's dance." Matt walked Sharonda to the dance floor.

After a few dances Matt suggested drinks and they went over to the bar.

"So I guess this is a good way to make up for our our little date you missed.

"Date, what date?"

"You forgot that fast. Sheesh I'm hurt." He said holding his chest.

"Oooh dinner at 5 meet me in the lobby I'm so sorry!!" Sharonda covered her mouth.

"Nah you forgot about me." Matt made a sad face.

"No seriously I'm sorry love. I was so busy I ended up getting off later than projected." She said.

"You gonna have to make it up to me then beautiful." Matt sipped his drink.

"What do you have in mind?" Sharonda asked.

"Well let's start with exchanging phone numbers and I'll hit you tomorrow." He handed his phone to Sharonda.

They exchanged numbers and walked to the car.

"Good night beautiful." Matt smiled.

"Good night." Sharonda replied.

Dajon

"Professor Le'aire thank you for your help I didn't know exactly what needed to be done." A student said.

"No problem I knew you'd get it." Dajon said.

"Yeah Professor Le'aire thank you." Another student winked.

She laughed. "You're welcome Xavier."

"Now that the semester is coming to an end we should celebrate." Xavier said.

"Celebrate what exactly?" Dajon asked.

"You're not my professor anymore so now we can grab a

drink? Remember I asked you before but you said I was your student." Xaiver smiled.

Xavier is a 6'3 well built 30 year old man who was finishing up his degree that he started years ago. He has dreads with butter cream brownskin, a beard and white pretty teeth. He was always dressed nice and neat, you could tell he was a businessman.

Dajon bit her lip as she was caught in a trance.

"Hey is that a yes or no?" Xavier waved his hand in front of Dajon.

"Oh, sorry, raincheck." She said.

"Here's my card just in case you change your mind beautiful." He said as other professors walked up.

"Have a good day ladies." Xaiver smiled.

"You know Ms. Le'aire you may want to be careful dating one of your students." Professor Potter said.

"Who said I was dating my student?" Dajon asked.

"It may be those tight skirts you parade around here in." Professor Read laughed.

"Wait, what?" Dajon stood.

"Yeah I've noticed the same thing." Professor Potter joined in laughter.

"It's very inappropriate. That may be how you dress down around the way with your "homegirls" but here that's not acceptable. We want to create an environment conducive to learning. The students..." Professor Read ranted.

Dajon interrupted, "listen very clearly, my very first semester here over 94% of my students passed the final with an A. 100% of my students passed the class without having to retake it. Unlike the 2 of your classes that had a 89% failing rate and most of your students came to my class this semester because they said that neither of you break it down for them to understand. Secondly, you walk around here saying how cute I look but yet you just insulted me with body shaming comments. Understand I'm a proud Black Woman and all of my curves that you secretly wish you had. So how about this ladies, you enjoy your winter break while I enjoy mine and worry about your students passing rate instead of failing the majority of the students of color here. You two disgust me." Dajon went into her office and closed the door in their faces.

Group text: Shit, I need a drink ladies. These bitches at this little part time tried it!! -Dajon

Group text: Chiiile, what happened?- Sharonda

Group text: These bitches hating they tell me my clothes are tight! I'm sorry God gave me a big ass and your ass is flat.

Group text: Wait, shout out to flat booties across America lol- Sharonda

Group text: Lol you have more booty than them- Dajon

Group text: You right lolol ya'll come to my place tonight.- Sharonda

Group text: Where is Marie anyway?- Dajon

Group text: Probably under somebody lol- Sharonda

Marie

Just then Marie knocked on Sharonda's door.

"Who is it?" Sharonda asked.

"Open the door girl!" Marie yelled.

Sharonda opened the door and Marie rushed in.

"Girl you still have on the clothes from last night, what happened??" Sharonda smirked.

"Girrrl, I need wine." Marie walked over to the couch.

Sharonda grabbed a bottle of wine and glasses.

"Girl I need the bottle." Marie said.

"Oh this is good tea!" Sharonda said flopping onto the couch.

"Ok so last night when ya'll left the party you know I stayed behind to ensure it all went well." Marie said.

"Ok yeah?" Sharonda asked.

"So this is how it went." Marie started.

Flashback

"Londyn, just take my car. Do NOT go anywhere but to the house. Don't be out anywhere!" Marie yelled.

"Ughh we just finished a fashion show and party where am I going to go? I'm going home." Londyn said.

"Alright boys good work tonight I'll see ya'll in a minute. "Eric dapped them up.

Marie stood by the door waiting for her uber.

"Hey Ms. Martin you good?" Eric asked.

"You can call me Marie." She smiled. "And yes I am just waiting for my uber."

"Ok well Marie you don't need to stand out here alone. I'll wait with you." Eric said.

"It's only a few minutes away. I'm fine. It's okay." She said.

"I told you I'd make sure nothing would happen to that beautiful smile. I'm going to wait." He said.

She smiled. "Thank you Eric."

"Oh you remember my name?" He smiled.

"Yeah I do, duh." Marie rolled her eyes.

"You want to sit in my truck it's a little windy?" He walked over to his SUV and opened the door.

"Well since you have the door opened, I guess I can't say no." Marie walked over and sat down.

Eric got in the car and turned on music.
. . . .

"Girrrrl can we skip all that, give me the good stuff! What happened? Ya'll slept together?" Sharonda grinned.

"Shut up let me finish girl. So we sat in the car sharing our past times and we have soooo much in common girl! But then girl he took that button down off and revealed those arms and tats." Marie continued.

Flashback

"Damn girl where's your uber?" Eric asked.

Marie snapped out of her trance. "Shoot you're right." She checked her app and the ride had been cancelled.

"Its cancelled wow." She dropped her phone in her lap.

"It's ok. He licked his lips. "I can take you home." He leaned forward to crank the car.

"Well...Ok thank you." Marie smiled.

"Don't worry I'm not going to stalk you beautiful." He laughed. His stomach growled. "Damn I'm hungry."

"Me tooooo but nothing is opened." Marie stretched.

"I can cook us something real quick." Eric said.

"Boy you can't cook." Marie pushed his arm.

"Watch me. If you don't mind I'll stop by my crib real quick, cook and then take you home." He said.

Marie looked at him.

"I'm not going to try anything girl or I can cook at your house but your man may not like that." He smirked.

Marie remembered Londyn would be at her place. "No we can stop by your place and I don't have a man." She said.

"That's surprising for someone so beautiful to be single, so am I." He said.

• •

"Girrrrrrrl you went to his house?! Nu un!" Sharonda exclaimed.

"Girl I know but Londyn was at my place and his was on the way to mine girl." Marie said.

"Aaaaaalright chiiiii..." Sharonda replied.

"Don't judge me." Marie sipped from the bottle.

"Ok. Chris Brown, baby please don't judge me honey" Sharonda sang.

They laughed.

"You right." Marie laughed harder.

"Go on with the story crazy." Sharonda said.

"Ok so we got to his house. Girl he lives in the city, city on like the 23rd floor. The view was gorgeous! Anyway, so he cooked eggs, sausage and pancakes." She said.

"Fam! That's sex food." Sharonda said.

"Girl, feed me!" Marie joked.

"Oop!! I'm hungry!" Sharonda joked.

"I need something to eat!" Marie laughed.

"Girl, you fed him didn't ya?" Sharonda grinned.

"Girl! Let me finish. So then he had his playlist playing and chiiiii "when we" remix by Tank came on." Marie continued.

Flashback

Marie was standing looking out of the floor to ceiling windows. Eric walked up behind her and she felt his breath hit the back of her neck. She took a deep breath.

"Do you want some more wine?" Eric asked.

Marie turned to face him and they stood face to face. She bit her bottom lip. "No I'm fine, thank you."

"Ok." Eric turned to take the bottle back to the kitchen.

Marie walked up behind him and placed her glass in the sink.

"You are so sexy." He smiled.

"Thank you Eric." Marie said.

"I like the way you say my name." He said.

"You're welcome Eric." Marie smirked.

"Alright let me take you home Ms. Martin before something gets started." Eric walked over to get his keys.

Marie walked up to Eric, "it already started."

Eric kissed Marie and picked her up and placed her on the counter.

They kissed more while he ran his hand up her dress until he felt her juices run down his fingers.

She let out a moan as he kissed down her neck.

End of Flashback

Sharonda sat with her mouth wide open. "Girrrrrl. You gave him the drawls!!" she exclaimed.

Marie put her hand on her forehead. "Yes girl, literally because I couldn't find my panties when I snuck out this morning. I blame the wine." She shook her head.

Sharonda burst out in laughter. "Girl bye."

Marie joined her with laughter. "It ain't funny."

Sharonda's door rang. "Who is it?"

"I know you see me on this camera. Let's go get some lunch I'm hungry."

"I can't." She said.

"Why?" Dajon asked.

"Marie here and on her way down. I have a date." She bit her lip.

"Oooooh! Mugs ain't tell me about that!" Dajon said.

"You right but I'ma tell both of ya'll when I get back. So I'll call you later." Sharonda said as they headed out the door.

"Um excuse me, where you are going with them booty shorts on?" Dajon asked.

"Girl!! These are not booty shorts." Sharonda said.

Marie tugged on her shorts. "Um, fam yes they are." She said.

"You know what, forget ya'll." Sharonda turned her head.

A black SUV pulled over.

"This must be my uber." Sharonda said.

Eric hopped out and walked up to Marie.

"Girl who is that?" Dajon whispered.

"Her new boo chiiile." Sharonda whispered.

Marie rolled her eyes at both Sharonda and Dajon as she hugged Eric. "Hi." She said.

"Hello Ms. Martin." He smiled. "Listen I was driving and saw it was you I promise I'm not stalking you."

Marie laughed. "I'm sure you're not but what's up?"

"You left my place so fast you forgot something." He held up her panties on his finger.

Marie's eyes got big and she snatched them and put them in her purse. "Oh my gosh!!" She exclaimed while Dajon and Sharonda laughed.

"Girrrrl she got the dick?!" Dajon exclaimed.

"Um shut up heffas! Don't you have a date. Bye!" She said to Sharonda and Dajon.

"I want a date like that." Dajon joked.

"I'll see ya'll later here's my uber." Sharonda laughed.

"Bye ya'll" Dajon walked away laughing.

"How you just hold those things up in front of everybody?" She asked.

"Them your girls I figured ya'll seen each other panties before." Eric laughed.

"It is not funny." Marie laughed.

"Why are you laughing then?" He asked.

"Whatever. Thank you for bringing my panties." She said.

"Well you look like you could use new clothes. So let me take you home forreal this time." Eric smiled.

"Fine. I'm going straight home." She climbed into his SUV.

Sharonda

Sharonda ignored her phone as she exited the car to meet with Matt.

"Hey beautiful." He greeted her.

"Hello sir." She smiled.

"Why so formal?" He asked.

"It's not. It's just something I say." She said as they walked along the river.

They continued to walk and get to know each other. He bought them ice cream and they sat on the bench.

"Dang your phone keeps ringing. Is it your boyfriend?" Matt asked.

"I'm completely single. So no it is not." Sharonda smiled.

"I'm just messing with you beautiful." He smiled and held his finger under her chin.

"So my afternoon is free, what do you want to do?" She asked.

"Hmm?" He thought.

"Keep it PG sir." Sharonda laughed.

"Hmmmmm." Matt smirked.

Matt got down and told Sharonda to climb on his back. "Let's just see where the day takes us." He said running with her on his back.

"Oh my gosh you are so silly!" Sharonda exclaimed.

He stopped when he got to the top of the hill. "What's going on?" Matt asked.

"It's food truck frenzy." Sharonda said.

"Let's try it." Matt walked forward.

"Which one?" She asked.

"All of them girl." He said.

Hours passed as the day went on. "What time is it?" She asked.

"7:30, why you have another date?" He smirked.

"Boy whatever but I do have to go." She said.

"Noooo, don't leave yet." He said.

Sharonda laughed. "You're such a baby."

Matt smiled and grabbed her hand and walked her to the edge of the river. "The sun always sets here and its beautiful." He wrapped his arm around Sharonda and stood behind her.

"You're right this is gorgeous." Her eyes lit up as she rubbed his hands.

They stood gaging at the sunset. Matt turned Sharonda towards him and they shared a passionate kiss.

Sharonda and Matt smiled then laughed at each other. They kissed again.

Sharonda phone went off with a text message. "Ok I really have to go." She said.

"Alright beautiful I hope you had fun today." Matt walked holding her hand.

"I did. I had a lot of fun." She said.

"I got you a Lyft." He opened the door. "Be safe." Matt kissed her again.

"Dang girl ya'll need a room!" The Lyft driver said.

"Um excuse you." Sharonda climbed inside. "Bye." She said to Matt.

Sharonda checked her messages and phone calls. It was all from one person, Cameron. Sharonda rolled her eyes, "what the hell is his problem?" She thought.

She exited the car and was about to enter the bar to meet with her girls.

"Yo Ronda" a voice called out.

She turned around to check to see the one person who would calle her by that nickname.

"That is you, what's up girl?" PJ hugged her.

"PJ hey what's up?" Sharonda returned the hug.

"You headed inside here?" He opened the door.

"I am." She entered in.

"Who you meeting with? Those crazy friends of yours." PJ said.

"First off we not crazy." Dajon said.

"I see its those crazy friends." He laughed.

"You tried it." Dajon said while Sharonda laughed.

"What's so funny?" Dajon asked.

"It was good to see you PJ." Sharonda grabbed Dajon to walk away.

PJ grabbed her hand. "You too Ronda." He smiled.

"I can't stand his cocky ass." Dajon said.

"I know I know." Sharonda said. "Calm down. I just happened to see him outside the bar. Anyways, where's Marie?" She asked.

"I don't know, hell that's your cousin, ya'll always late." Dajon laughed.

"Oop, you tried it." Sharonda said cutting her eye to the bar where PJ was sitting.

PJ sat with his friends and turned his seat outward to face Sharonda's table. He licked his lips and glanced over towards her.

He sent a drink to her table. "That gentleman there at the bar sent this over to you." The waitress said.

"Thank you." Sharonda smiled and looked down at the drink.

"Nawl don't look down." Dajon said.

"Huh?" Sharonda asked.

Marie walked in. "Sorry I'm late ya'll what I missed?" Marie asked.

"Nothing girl the live band just got here." Sharonda said.

"Girl so on the way over here I had a hoe bath." Marie ducked her head.

"What happened?!" Dajon said.

Sharonda sipped her glass as she brought her attention back from PJ. "Fam spill it!" She exclaimed.

"Ok, you remember Eric from earlier?" Marie asked.

"Yeah, c'mon." Dajon responded.

"Ok we were in the car riding home and oh my God some kind of way my dress came up and I didn't make it home again!" Marie said.

"Wait a minute, again!?" Dajon exclaimed.

"Wheeeeet?" Sharonda said.

"Yes ya'll, the dick got me." Marie shook her head in shame.

Dajon and Sharonda burst out laughing.

"It's not funny." Marie pouted.

"Yeah it is." Sharonda continued to laugh.

"Ladies, ladies, a round on us." PJ said with his friends behind him.

"No we're fine, thank you." Sharonda said.

"Yes, we want that round. I need that round." Marie said.

"Yeah free drinks for us." Dajon smirked.

"I'm gonna go to the bathroom." Sharonda walked away.

The band began playing music as PJ's friends pulled up chairs and got drinks. PJ walked towards the bathroom. Sharonda was coming out and they bumped into each other.

"You look good gorgeous." PJ smiled.

"Thank you PJ." Sharonda smiled.

"So you really going to act like you don't miss me right now?" He asked.

"Are you serious?" She asked.

"Yes am I wrong?" He smiled.

Sharonda laughed. "You think you are so fine." She said.

"I mean I like to think you do too." He smirked.

"Ugh, I can't stand your conceited ass." She rolled her eyes.

PJ stepped up on her. "Oh really?" He asked.

"Really!" She replied.

"Really?" PJ moved closer.

"Really! Back up." She said.

PJ kissed her as they went into the bathroom.

"Stop PJ." Sharonda moaned.

"You sure you want me to stop?" He asked.

"Yes, I can't go back down this road with you." Sharonda adjusted herself.

PJ is Sharonda's ex that everyone hated. He was cocky and conceited tall 6'1 brother with beautiful curly hair and light brown eyes. He had such a strong fashion sense and always smelled like a bottle of Men's Versace. It was her favorite smell to buy him. Although cocky he was also a charming sweetheart that no one else got to see but Sharonda. He would always get her flowers and Starbucks it was her favorite. They broke up because he wasn't ready for the type of commitment Sharonda was asking for. After 2 years of dating Sharonda couldn't do it anymore. She knew he wasn't going to change and she accepted it.

"What road Ronda?" PJ licked his lips.

"Us meeting up to have sex, I finally got you out of my system and I cannot do this again. And stop calling me that you know I hate it. Call me Sharonda or by Shae, my nickname but not Ronda." Sharonda said.

"But did we meet here for sex? No Shae, we just happened to be in the same place at the same time." He said.

"Well listen either way we're not doing this anymore." She

said.

"Does this have anything to do with that nigga I saw you with last night?" He asked.

"So that was you staring last night. I thought you looked familiar." She said.

"So it does then." PJ backed up. "I respect you but he'll never give you what we had."

"And what did we have PJ? Besides you not communicating with me and staying out all night and me not knowing what the hell you were doing, what did we have?" Sharonda crossed her arms.

PJ smirked. "You mad?" He touched her arms. "Don't act like we ain't have a great love together. I miss you foreal." He said.

"No I'm not mad. And don't say that you just saw me with someone and feel some type of way." She said.

"I could really care less about him. I'm just saying." He said.

"Bye PJ." Sharonda walked out of the bathroom and back to the table.

PJ returned afterwards and sat next to her. Sharonda let out a sigh.

"You good sis?" Dajon asked.

"I'm great." Sharonda said sarcastically.

"Aye shots for everyone." PJ's friend came back to the table. "A toast to a good life!" everyone drank their shot.

After a few drinks and hours later Sharonda was ready to go.

"Ya'll I'm gonna turn in." Sharonda said.

"Nooo, don't leave us." A wasted Dajon said.

"Girl you drunk you need to leave as well." Sharonda laughed.

"Nope I'm good." Dajon laughed.

"I got her cousin. Be safe and text us when you get home." Marie said.

Marie got a text. It was a picture of Eric and him making a silly face." She laughed. "On second thought we're all going to leave." Marie stood.

"Shae?" PJ called.

"What's up?" She asked.

"You really gonna leave like that?" PJ asked.

"I said goodbye." She turned to walk to the car.

PJ followed behind her as Marie and Dajon climbed into her truck.

"I really do miss you." He said.

Sharonda climbed into her truck. "PJ you're the ex-boyfriend, just play your part." She closed her door and drove off.

Chapter Three- This Could Be

Sharonda checked herself in the mirror and grabbed her reading glasses.

"Get out of my kitchen fixing cereal and shit. That's not what this is boy." She said.

"Damn a nigga can't get breakfast before he leaves?" He asked.

"Hell no you can't and it's not breakfast its 2 o'clock negro." She laughed.

He laughed. "Smartass mouth," he smacked her butt.

"Aye, watch your hands." She grabbed his keys and handed them to him.

"You so mean." He walked towards the door.

Sharonda rolled her eyes. "Bye PJ." She smirked.

"Bye Ronda." He laughed knowing she hated to be called that.

"Ugh can't stand that lil boy." Sharonda said as she hopped on the counter.

She checked emails for work and her text messages. Her phone began to ring.

"Hello?" She answered.

"Well hello beautiful." Matt said.

"Hi Matt how are you?" She asked.

"I'm good I was wondering what were you doing right now?" He asked.

"Just following up on a few things for work. What about you?" She asked.

"You're always working. Come go with me." He suggested.

"Where?" Sharonda smiled.

"Now that would ruin the surprise." He smiled.

"Um, what time?" Sharonda asked.

"30 minutes meet me on 5th and Ave." He ended the call.

"Sheesh hanging up all in my face." Sharonda looked at the phone.

Sharonda wore black workout pants, with red and black nikes, and a red crop top hoodie. It complimented her already done natural make-up. She pulled her behind her ears and headed to meet Matt.

He walked up with grey joggers, a black fitted shirt, with black nikes and a grey fitted hat.

"Well this is out of the norm for you." Sharonda smiled.

"I could say the same for you beautiful." He smiled and hugged her. "You smell good girl."

"Thank you. You too Matt." She blushed.

"Oh, look at you blushing. Did I do that?" He joked.

"Whatever...so what are we doing today?" Sharonda asked.

"I figured we could go in here to get a workout in and get to know each other and afterwards have a smoothie." Matt opened the door to the gym.

Marie

Marie sat in her bed going over the layout of her new website with her designer. "See how that's kind of difficult to do if they want to customize it. I'd rather we be able to just type a code for them to be able to click the button and it pops up." She said.

"I see what you mean Marie and that can be done." The web designer replied.

"Ok great. Thanks so much." She said.

"No problem we'll fix it and send you a complete email when its complete. Thanks for using our services." The web designer replied.

"Sure. Thank you!" Marie smiled and ended the call. She closed her Macbook and looked up at Eric who was standing in a towel fresh out of the shower.

"Why are you just standing there?" She asked.

"I like hearing you handle your business. I like your drive." He smiled walking over and sitting next to her.

She straddled him. "I thought you like when I ride." She rested her arms on his neck.

He chuckled. "Yeah you're right I do." He rested his arms on the small of her back. "But I like that you're goal oriented and have that business mindset." He pecked her lips.

"Aww thank you I try." She smiled.

"You silly babe." He pecked her lips once more. "You have to get up though because if not something is going to get started and I'll miss my flight." He squeezed her butt.

"Okaaay." Marie made a sad face.

"Don't be like that while I'm gone we'll stay in contact don't worry I told you that." Eric said getting dressed.

"I know." She said.

"Oh so what you're saying is you're going to miss me?" He smirked.

"No I'm not." Marie stuck her tongue out.

Eric sucked her tongue and they shared a deep kiss. "I'm going to miss that." She smiled.

Eric smacked her on her butt. "I'm going to miss that." He smiled.

She nodded her head. "I know." They laughed.

"No butt foreal I just like hanging out with you and what we've developed over these few months while I've been home has been amazing." Eric said holding Marie's hand.

"I can agree with that." She blushed.

"Well listen I'm going to head out before I miss my flight." Eric said walking to the door.

"Wait." Marie grabbed his hands and began to pray for his safety. She finished the prayer and the both of them said, "Amen."

"You're so sweet. Thank you babe." They kissed and they opened the door to see Dajon.

"Oh so he stay here?" Dajon said smiling.

"You nosey!" Marie laughed.

"Byeeeeee!" Dajon laughed as Eric left.

"Girl what are you doing over here anyway?" Marie asked walking to the living room.

"I was just out this way sh..shopping." Dajon stuttered.

"Lies you tell. What's going on?" Marie asked.

"I was just at lunch with Derek." Dajon said.

"Oh okay how'd that go?" Marie asked.

"I love him but he be doing some off the wall shit." Dajon teared up.

"Its hard but you can't help who you love." Marie hugged Dajon.

"Yeah and I just found out I'm 6 weeks pregnant." Dajon covered her face.

"Oh honey." Marie grabbed tissue.

"We hadn't spoke in about 2 weeks. I just needed some time and I met up with him just to discuss some things in our relationship." Dajon said.

"Wow honey are you going to tell him?" She asked.

"I don't know I don't want to deal with his crazy bipolar ass anymore." Dajon cried.

"But you're pregnant so eventually he'll need to know." Marie said.

"I know but he doesn't even take care of his other kids." Dajon said.

"Um, how many does he have?" Marie asked.

"3 by 3 different women." Dajon cried.

"Damn sis! I feel for you love." Marie said.

"I know." Dajon continued to cry.

Chapter Four - My Bestfriend

Marie walked out of the bathroom as her phone began to ring.

"Hello?" She answered.

"Hi beautiful how are you today?" Eric asked.

"I'm great love just laying across my bed I'm so tired." Marie looked into her phone.

"Ahh, you aight get your butt up so you can go workout." Eric laughed.

"I'm going to get up I promise." She laughed. "How are things going for you?"

"They're good actually. The show went good for Ty tonight and thank God he just chilling so I can just enjoy my time talking to you." He smiled.

Marie blushed. "I miss you." She said.

"I miss you too. I'll be back home in a little while though. The tour ends in London." He said.

"I can't wait until I'm actually there at a fashion show featuring my pieces." Marie day dreamed.

"It's definitely going to happen babygirl. I believe in you."

He smiled.

"Thank you boo." Marie smiled.

"Yeah for sure I actually have been giving your card out to everyone I could." He said.

"I was wondering where all these new followers were coming from." She laughed.

"Yeah you know I got you babe." Eric said.

Marie and Eric continued to talk until it was 2am in South Korea.

"Babe I have to be up in a few hours go workout foreal now girl." Eric said.

"Okaaaay. I'm going to go now. I'll talk to you later." Marie propped her phone on her dresser.

"Better stop before I get you to give me a strip tease." Eric smirked.

Marie laughed and winked her eye as she removed her bra underneath her shirt.

"You play too much girl." Eric said.

Marie laughed. "Hurry up and come back to me." She said.

"I got you babygirl." Eric blew Marie a kiss.

Marie kissed her phone. "Bye." The call ended.

Marie continued to get dressed and her phone began to ring. "Hey whats up babe?" She asked.

"We forgot to pray babygirl." Eric said.

He lead the prayer and Marie stood by and listened. She admired how he would take charge and lead them in prayer. She loved his relationship with Christ and that meant everything to her.

"Amen." They said together and the call ended.

Sharonda

"Finally I get a smoothie." Sharonda joked.

"I let you win." Matt said.

"Nah you definitely lost fair and square." Sharonda bragged.

"I'm 6'4 you're 5'4 do you really think you can beat me?" He flexed his muscles.

Sharonda felt his muscles and pushed his arms, "they alright." She laughed.

"Oh you just gonna shade me like that? That's alright. Me and my hurt little feelings will be alright." Matt put his head down and sipped his smoothie.

"Aww poor baby." Sharonda caressed his bearded face.

"Nah don't try to be my friend now." Matt turned his face.

Sharonda turned his face back to her and smiled, "you mad at me?" She asked.

"Don't look at me like that girl!" Matt exclaimed.

"What I didn't do anything?" Sharonda asked.

Matt slid her chair closer to him. He leaned in, "keep playing with me." He said in a sexy deep tone.

Sharonda bit her lip and smiled. "Don't play with me." She said.

Matt leaned in and they shared a sweet kiss.

"Well, well, well that's why we can't find her she always out with this one." Marie said walking up on Sharonda and Matt.

"Hey boo!" She reached for Marie and Dajon.

"Nawl don't boo me we've been trying to get you for the past week." Marie said.

"Girl I don't know what you're talking about." Sharonda shot Marie a look.

Marie squinted to understand the look.

"Mmhmm well introduce us." Dajon said.

"Im sorry. Matt this is Marie, my cousin and Dajon, my best-friend. They are my sisters from another Mister." Sharonda said.

Matt stood and shook their hands. "Nice to meet you both, I'm Matt." He said.

"Well damn. You're really tall." Marie said.

"Nice to meet you as...as well." Dajon struggled and ran off to the bathroom.

"What's wrong with her?" Sharonda asked.

"You know she hasn't worked out in a while girl." Marie lied. "Well hit us later I'm gonna go check on her." She said.

"Well I'll come too." Sharonda started.

"No, no stay with your date. I'll go alone. It's cool." Marie hesitated.

"No. I'm coming. That's my bestfriend." Sharonda insisted.

"Ah she's coming back. See she's fine." Marie smiled.

"Hey girl you good?" Sharonda asked.

"Oh yeah just ate something bad." Dajon said.

"Ok well I guess I'll talk to ya'll later." Sharonda said.

"Alright see ya girl." Dajon said.

Sharonda and Matt pulled up to her loft apartment building. They sat in the car talking.

"You know we could always have this conversation inside though right?" Matt asked.

"Ha you funny." Sharonda smirked.

"Nah not like that but foreal like this is going good I don't want it to be over yet." Matt held her hand.

Sharonda looked him in the eye. Matt put his finger underneath her chin and licked his lips. Matt stared into Sharonda's eyes with his bright brown eyes, his caramel skin glistening in the sun light and his full lips as he moved closer to Sharonda. She leaned in for a kiss.

Afterwards they shared a laughed. "You silly girl." Matt said.

"I'm kind of shy." Sharonda said.

"Lies. There's nothing shy about you." He kissed her again.

"Ok I should get inside." Sharonda said.

Matt walked her to the door and gave her hug and one more kiss.

Upon entering the building she was greeted by the doorman.

"Hi Sharonda these are for you." He said.

It was a large bouquet of red roses. The card read "thank you for blessing me with that gorgeous smile today. This is for you and your friends on me. –Matt"

It was a card for her favorite SPA. Sharonda walked into her loft. "Hey google call Lyft rider."

"Hello?" Matt answered.

"Thank you. You are so sweet! I love my roses!" Sharonda exclaimed.

Matt smiled. "Anything for you beautiful. I'm just trying to be your bestfriend."

Sharonda smiled. "What does that mean?" She asked.

"I know how ya'll women are about relationships. You want a bestfriend before a boyfriend. I'm just trying to be your bestfriend." He said.

Sharonda blushed. "See you get it." They laughed. "I really do want a bestfriend before a boyfriend." She said.

"Well let me be your bestfriend." Matt said.

"We're working on it." Sharonda smiled. "Roses are my favorite flowers by the way."

"Well there's definitely more where that came from ma'am. So I think the next date should be tacos and drinks. Are you down for that?" He asked.

"Yes that's perfect!" She smiled.

"Ok well I'll see you soon beautiful." Matt smiled.

"Ok bye." The call ended.

Chapter Five-Wasted Off You

Sharonda sat on her counter cheesing and playing with her roses as a call came into her place. She looked at the camera to see that it was PJ.

"What do you want?" She answered.

"Let me up." PJ said.

"Why?" She asked.

"Let's talk." He said.

Sharonda buzzed the door so he could enter. She waited for the knock on the door and let him in.

"Come in." She said.

"Hello to you too Ronda." He smirked.

"What do you want you know I hate being called that." Sharonda rolled her eyes.

"My bad Sharonda nice roses." He said.

"Thank you." She walked around the island and grabbed an apple. "So why are you here?" She asked.

"Damn I can't visit a friend?" He asked.

"No, not if it's not an emergency." Sharonda said.

"Let me ask you a question." He leaned against the sofa.

"Yes?" She answered.

"You don't miss me even a little bit?" He asked.

"No I don't we've been through this already." She sighed and turned towards the window that overlooked the city skyline.

He walked up behind her. "Say it to my face."

Sharonda turned around. "No I don't miss your dumbass."

He laughed. "You're so stubborn I can't stand you." He said.

"Then why are you here?" Sharonda crossed her arms.

"You always trying to be mad." PJ said as he uncrossed her arms. "I'm just playing with you."

"If you have nothing foreal to talk about you can leave." Sharonda walked away.

"Alexa play Tank When We." He said.

"No, what the hell?" Sharonda asked. "I'm serious with you!" Sharonda exclaimed.

"That's why our shit didn't work you always fucking mad!" He said.

"You're always making me fucking mad! You and your dumbass remarks." She got in his face.

He grabbed her face and kissed her. "No I'm not doing this with you PJ." Sharonda moved her face.

He kissed her neck and picked her up and continued to kiss and lick on her until they made it to the couch. He stretched her arms out and kissed down her body until he reached her love top.

Sharonda squirmed around, PJ in turn removed all of her

clothes and lifted her on top of his shoulders. She ran her hands through his curly hair as her juices flowed into his mouth. He kept going until he felt her legs begin to shake. He placed her face down ass up over the edge of the couch. He then grabbed her ass and stuck his face in it. Sharonda let out a soft moan as she played around her clit. He reached around and put his hand on top of hers continuing to massage her clit and eat her ass. Sharonda's moans grew louder as she reached her peak once more. He kissed her back up to her neck.

Sharonda helped PJ remove his clothes while she massaged him. She whispered in his ear, "I can't stand you."

"Shit I can't stand your ass either." He said while smacking her ass.

He lay back on her bear fur rug as she climbed on top. She bounced on top of him as he let out a small moan. He cupped her breast in his hand and sucked them to keep from "sounding like a bitch," is what he would always say while they were together. Sharonda thought of how she would fix that. She turned around and grabbed his ankles and rode nice and slow and then picked up the pace finding just the right rhythm to match him. PJ smacked her ass and moaned.

Deeper by Silk came on as well as Meeting in my Bedroom. By the end they had finished 3 rounds. Sharonda wrapped herself in a towel and went into the bathroom.

PJ stood stared at Sharonda in the mirror. "What?" She asked from the bathroom.

"Nothing." He began getting dressed. "Since you can't stand me I'm going to leave." He said.

"Ok bye." She said dryly.

"Damn." He chuckled.

"You can't stand me either remember?" She asked walking out of the bathroom.

"Nah that's all you but whatever." He started towards the door.

"Don't start that." Sharonda said.

"Start what?" He asked.

"This back and forth stuff. You say you want me, then you don't. I don't want to play that game with you." She said.

"I'm not playing a game Ronda you already know how I feel about you." He said.

"No I don't, tell me PJ how do you feel?" She stood with her hands on her hip.

"Man you already know I don't have to tell you." He said.

"Exactly what I thought. Goodbye." Sharonda rolled her eyes.

"Ugly ass flowers I hope they die." He said.

Sharonda laughed. "You mad or nah?" She asked.

"3 rounds say I can never be mad." PJ smirked.

"Whatever get out." Sharonda opened the door.

"Next time I want it in the shower." He said kissing her lips.

"It won't be a next time." Sharonda pushed him back.

PJ laughed as he walked off. "Yeah okay."

Dajon

"Alright everyone's grades will be posted on Monday." Dajon said.

"Hello Professor Le'aire." Xavier walked from the top of the stairs.

Dajon smiled. "Well hello sir and how are you?" She asked.

"I'm great. Now about that raincheck?" He smiled.

"I'll be busy reading essays so I can post grades love I'm sorry." Dajon gathered her things.

"Alright what about Monday morning Breakfast?" Xavier asked.

"Umm..." Dajon pondered.

"Brunch? Lunch? Dinner? I'm not giving up." He smiled.

Dajon laughed. "You know you're very persistent."

"With a woman like you I have to be." Xavier opened the door for her.

"What does that mean?" She asked walking out to the car.

"That means you're very beautiful and I will not let your beauty out of my site." He walked with her.

"Cute. So what's your story?" She asked.

"Let me take you to dinner tonight and we can discuss all of that." He opened her car door.

"I really can't right now." Dajon said.

"Listen how about this...put my number in your phone and then when you're free and have time hit me. I won't rush you but you will be mine." He smiled.

"Cocky." Dajon smirked.

"Not at all I just know a blessing when I see it Professor."

Dajon was taken back by that comment but knew she was not in a place for a new relationship, she was pregnant, trying to determine if she'd keep it or not, would she tell Derek and how he'd respond, and after everything they'd been through she knew her heart just wasn't available.

Dajon smiled. "Ok that was a good line." She said.

"Not a line just the truth." Xaiver flashed his pearly white teeth.

"Ok just put your number in my phone." She handed him her phone.

"Alright its in there and any time Professor Le'aire." Xaiver said.

"Just call me Dajon. Enjoy your break." She climbed into her.

Dajon sent a text to the group: "what ya'll doing tonight?" she asked.

Group text: "I'm just working on some pieces and I have an appearance to make downtown." Marie said.

Group text: "Where at?" Dajon asked.

Group text: "This new lounge in town. Ya'll should pull up." Marie said.

Group text: "Ok where the hell is Sharonda?" Dajon asked.

Group text: "Girl acting brand new." Marie replied.

Hours later they were out at the lounge. Dajon and Marie were out on the dance floor dancing when Derek walked in with his friends. He spotted Dajon and sent over drinks for her and Marie.

"Free drinks! I'll take it." Marie cheered.

"Girl he just trying to get my attention." Dajon said.

"So you not gonna take it?" Marie asked.

"Well I kind of can't." Dajon said.

"I'll take your shot and you can have wine." Marie said.

Sharonda walked up to them. "I don't appreciate ya'll talking about me like that in the group text." She said.

"Heeeey!!" Dajon exclaimed.

"Hey boo!" Sharonda returned the excitement.

"Hi cousin." Sharonda leaned over to Marie.

"Nu un I'm mad. You been MIA. I hope this new nigga got good dick." Marie said.

"Ooo I can't stand you!" Sharonda laughed as they shared a hug.

"I missed my friend!" Dajon said.

"That's bestfriend." Sharonda said.

"You're right. I missed you bestfriend." Dajon said.

"I missed ya'll too. I just been so busy with work." Sharonda said.

"Excuse me ladies." Derek said.

Sharonda rolled her eyes as she knew more than Marie about the history of Dajon and Derek's relationship.

Throughout their relationship Derek has done some very harsh things to Dajon. He blacked her eye and busted her lip; he left her stranded in New Jersey all because she decided to speak to a guy she hadn't seen since high school. He said that they were creeping on the low together. Sharonda had to drive to pick her up. He embarrassed her at a luncheon her job was putting on. They argue all the time and he mentally and emotionally abuses her. He's had a baby with another woman while with Dajon and continues to cheat on her.

Marie leaned over to Sharonda and whispered, "is that the Derek she been tripping over?"

Sharonda responded, "yeah that's that fuck nigga." She said loud.

"I can fucking hear you but I didn't come over here for that. What's up Dae?" He asked.

"What's up?" Dajon asked.

"You looking real nice tonight." He said.

"Thank you. You too." Dajon said finishing her wine.

"Can we talk?" Derek asked.

"No." Dajon grabbed another glass of wine.

"Ha, she told you." Sharonda laughed.

Derek shot Sharonda with an evil look. "Please?" He asked.

"She said no." Sharonda said.

Derek walked off mad. Dajon was almost in tears and finished her glass of wine and went for another.

"Ok you should slow down." Marie said.

"No let her be free. She needs it." Sharonda said.

"No she really needs to slow down. Emotional drinking is not good." Marie said.

"I'm good." Dajon continued to drink.

It was about 3 am and the lounge was letting out. Dajon, Sharonda and Marie were laughing while climbing into Lyft.

Derek walked over to Dajon before she could get in and grabbed her arm. "Baby I miss you and I love you. Can we please just talk?" he asked.

"You guys go ahead and I'll catch up." She said to Marie and Sharonda.

"Thank you for giving me time." Derek said.

"Yeah what's up?" Dajon asked.

"Wait are you tipsy?" Derek asked.

"A little. But what's up?" Dajon asked.

"I just feel like we've been together too long to just let it go." Derek said as they walked to the car.

"Derek I'm just tired of the back and forth. You always fucking up and then want to work it out." Dajon got into his car.

Derek entered the driver side and began driving. "Why is it always me?" He asked.

"Because what have I done besides be faithful, loyal, supportive and motivating to you. I cut off a lot of niggas for you even men who were just my friends." Dajon vented.

"I cut off people for you too though babe." Derek said.

"Derek who was the chick that was in my dm on IG? She said she was your girl and I was the side piece. How many times has that happened? Let's not forget when you were pressed for money who gave you the money to get back home? When your father passed away who was there for you?" Dajon began crying.

"You're right baby. I am sorry. I need to do better and I will if you just give us a try again. We've been together 4 years baby like its always been us. I just can't let you go." He said.

Dajon continued to cry.

"Baby say something." He grabbed her hands.

"I love you Derek but its like I just I don't want to keep getting hurt by you. Like do you realize the shit you do hurts? It breaks my fucking heart." Dajon said.

"Baby you know what let me do something to make it up to you." Derek said as he kissed her tears.

Derek continued to kiss her and with each soft touch he would utter, "I'm sorry." He parked his car and slid her panties to the side. "I love you and I just want to make it up to you. I owe you this baby."

Dajon's head fell back as she cried more. "It's like I'm wasted off your love. I just can't say no to you."

Derek reached up and locked his hands with Dajon's hands. He pulled her on top of him.

"I love you just don't hurt me anymore please." She said.

Derek wiped her eyes and pecked her lips. "I love you and I won't Dae." He said.

Chapter Six-That Magic

Marie

Marie, Dajon and Sharonda sat in the living room of Marie's place.

"Yall where are we going for this next season's Vacation?" Dajon asked.

"Girl unlike you two heffas I work everyday so I have to put in the request and ya'll know my mom's coming I wanted to take some time off to hang out with her." Sharonda said.

"True I feel it. My momma coming too. We should take them to the spa or something." Marie said.

"Oh that would be great." Sharonda and Marie clinked their glasses together.

"Well I guess I'll have to go on my own vacation with Derek." Dajon said.

Sharonda rolled her eyes. "Yeah...ok." She said.

"What? Why all of that?" Dajon asked.

"Why are you still with this man? He ain't shit. He's a true f boy." Sharonda said.

"Why are you judging him?" Dajon crossed her arms.

"How am I judging him? These are facts. This mofo mentally abuses you, ya'll argue and fight all the time, and he's cheated on you more than once, twice, hell 10 times." Sharonda ranted.

"Wait I'm going to stop you right there. I'm not saying anything about your man oh wait you don't have one so don't say shit about my man." Dajon said.

"Right your man and everyone else's too." Sharonda got up and went into the bathroom.

Marie stood off to the side on the phone as the argument went on. "Babe, these two just went in on each other. The tension so thick up in here." She said.

"Shut the hell up." Dajon said.

"Oh no don't bring it here. Your problem is not with me it's with your bestfriend." Marie said.

"Baby chill don't get into that." Eric said.

"I'm good I'm just waiting to see you." Marie rolled her eyes.

"You know what fuck both of ya'll. Ya'll always taking each other side." Dajon grabbed her things and headed out.

"Her dramatic ass get on my nerves. Gon say I'm judging her man. Like why would I judge him or anyone for that matter. I'm just stating the facts. You're mad because I'm bringing the shit to your face. Like fuck outta here!" Sharonda vented.

"Calm down fam maybe she's just emotional because of the bs she's been going through." Marie said.

"Like we all not going through stuff? I'm there for her all the time and have her best interest at heart. Like if you only knew all of the messed up stuff this man has done to her and I really believe he has put his hands on her more than that one time but she won't leave him anyway." Sharonda went off.

"Babe let me call you back ok?" Marie asked.

"Sure that's fine take care of that. Check your phone when you get a chance though." Eric said.

"Ok I will." Marie said.

"Um I know you not about to hang up on me without blowing me a kiss?" Eric asked.

"Babe not right now." Marie proceeded into the kitchen.

"I'm not hanging up until I get a kiss." Eric laughed.

Marie quickly pecked her phone, "There happy." She laughed.

"Yep I am." Eric sent her a kiss and the call ended.

Marie placed her phone on the counter and walked over to Sharonda. "Girl I understand what you're saying and you just want the best for your friend. Trust me I've gone through this and with some people you have to just let them go through before you can say something." She said.

"Dick-matized ass." Sharonda said.

Marie busted out laughing.

Sharonda laughed. "What's funny?" She asked.

"Because your ass just burst out with "dick-matized." Marie laughed.

"Girl." Sharonda said as they continued to laugh.

"But some people can't handle the truth even when its right before their eyes. Like you're just telling her the truth

and looking out for her but that man has a hold on her."
Marie said.

"Dickmatized." Sharonda said as she and Marie laughed.

Hours past as they watched their favorite movies and tv
series, Grown-ish, Waiting to Exhale and Living single.

Sharonda was napping meanwhile Marie remembered to
check her phone. She went into her email and the first
email had the subject line: a gift for my baby.

She smiled and opened the email. The email read "its been
damn near 2 months since we were last near each other and
because I miss you so much you're coming to one of the last
shows of the tour. So bring you and your friends out to Cali,
Ty Dolla, Chris Brown, Tory Lanez, etc. I'll see you soon
baby."

Marie began screaming. Sharonda woke up in a panic.
"What?! What's going on!?" she asked.

"We're going to Cali! Eric has invited us out for one of the
last shows!" Marie screamed.

Sharonda joined in on her screaming. "Seeing both of my
men at the same time!!" Sharonda day dreamed. She loved
Ty Dolla Sign and Tory Lanez.

"Ok so invite Dajon I want her to come and I'll invite 2
more people." Marie said.

"Hmph." Sharonda rolled her eyes.

"Don't do all that just make sure that girl come." Marie
said.

"Look at you, all giggly eyes over that man." Sharonda
joked.

"Girl just wait until I see him. He's got that magic!" Marie fell onto Sharonda.

"Eww. That is too much information." Sharonda frowned.

Marie laughed. "Not like that but I mean everything about this man was made especially for me."

"Aww that's sweet but tell the truth it's like that." Sharonda cocked her head to the side.

"You right." Marie nodded and they laughed.

Sharonda

The next day Sharonda was sitting in her office reviewing notes for her meeting.

"Hey Sharonda, I wanted to speak with you before the day ended." Ashley the new employee said.

"Ok sure. Come on in." Sharonda motioned with her hand.

Ashley walked in and sat down. "I kind of have a personal question to ask you." She whispered.

Sharonda giggled a bit wondering what she was going to ask. "Yes ma'am?" She asked.

"How do you deal with it?" Ashley asked pointing to the inside of her hand.

Sharonda got up and closed her door. "Girl it is not easy. I get so tired of being asked about my hair or stared at all day when we go to these meetings." She said.

"Oh my gosh I mean I was in the bathroom and 2 of the women in there asked me was my hair real and how did it become so straight. Like wtf you don't even know me like that!" Ashley said.

Sharonda laughed. "Girl I already know." She said.

"When I saw you and that you were black I said Lord thank

you Jesus one like me." Ashley laughed.

"There's one more here he works in Code Enforcement and when he first came on they tried to make him cut his dreads. He really almost quit it was a big deal some people got fired." Sharonda said.

"Oh wow." Ashley replied.

"Girl I could tell you so many stories but I just don't let them get to me. Let's get to this meeting though before the day ends." Sharonda opened her door.

"Thanks so much Sharonda." Ashley said.

"No problem." She smiled.

Sharonda entered the meeting space just as it was beginning.

"Nice of you to join us Sharonda." Howie said.

Sharonda smiled and winked her eye at Ashley. The meeting continued and it came time for Sharonda to give her input.

"Well I think we should just apply for the grant and work as a team to get it done before the deadline instead of putting it on one individual. I understand the load of writing grants as I have done so previously. I've taken the liberty in breaking it into 3 sections." Sharonda passed folders down with the information.

"As you'll see in the packet one is for technology, training, and..." Sharonda was interrupted.

"Excuse me Sharonda." Howie said.

"Yes?" She asked.

"I just noticed your nails, last they were green and now they're white." Howie said.

"I'm sorry what's the relevance to Environmental Health?" She asked.

"Well we want our owners and constituents to practice safe food handling do you think it wise to have nails?" He asked.

"Well if you'll notice I never go into any actual restaurants I'm usually working out an office, in a meeting, or training. Also regarding our female employees as long as gloves are worn at all times according to the food code they are allowed to wear nails. Check 2.2 it's clearly stated." Sharonda smirked.

Howie sat quietly as everyone gleamed at him. Sharonda cocked her head to the side as to say "what now bitch?"

"It's almost 5 o'clock everyone. Have a great weekend and see you next week!" She said and exited the room.

Ashley walked by her office. "Wow" she said.

"Girl he's an asshole for sure. He's sexist and racist but its time to go now. Have a great weekend." Sharonda said hoping on the elevator.

Sharonda exited the elevator and to her surprise Matt was standing with yellow roses by the door. "Hi sweetie. These are so beautiful!" Sharonda smiled.

"Hello beautiful." He hugged her and handed her the roses.

"Thank you. You're so sweet." Sharonda pecked Matt's lips.

"I missed you sort of kind of." Matt said holding the door open for Sharonda.

"Ohh sort of?" She asked.

"Yep." Matt opened the door to the car and Sharonda climbed in.

"So what's for dinner tonight?" Sharonda asked.

"I thought we could do something a little different." Matt said.

"Where are we going?" She asked.

"Just sit back and enjoy the ride baby." Matt smiled.

2 hours later Sharonda woke up to a big beautiful house located on the countryside.

She stretched as Matt parked. "Where are we?" she asked.

"Nice of you to join me finally sleepy head." He laughed.

"Whatever. Who's house is this?" She asked climbing out of the car.

"Let me get that door hold up." Matt said rushing to her side.

"This house is so beautiful." She said.

Matt pushed the doorbell. "Matthew!" The woman screamed.

"Hey baby sis, what's up?" He threw his arms around her.

"Hi I'm Tierra." She said to Sharonda.

"Hi I'm Sharonda." They shook hands.

"Come on in and meet my parents. They have some big announcement to make and wanted us here." He grabbed Sharonda's hand and walked into the dining room.

Matt greeted his parents and introduced Sharonda to his mother and father. His mother immediately embraced Sharonda. "She is beautiful Matt." His mother said.

"I hope my son is treating you right." His father said.

Sharonda smiled, "he's doing alright." She joked.

"Just alright?" Matt asked.

"Yeah you aight." Everyone laughed.

"You know what, she doesn't let you have your way. I like her." Tierra laughed.

Everyone talked over dinner and got to know Sharonda a little more. "Come on let me show you around." Matt stood from the table.

"Girl you got this man pulling out your seat and shit. Oops I'm sorry ma. I mean this nigga acting sprung. Ok girrrl." Tierra exaggerated.

"Shut up T." Matt laughed.

Matt and Sharonda came to the last place on the list which was a view that looked out over the landscape. "Your parents' place is gorgeous. You really grew up here?" She asked.

"We moved here when I was like 16. My dad didn't want to live in the city anymore." Matt sat on the edge of the bridge and pulled Sharonda to him and wrapped his arms around her waist.

"So why did you bring me to meet your parents?" Sharonda asked.

"I mean if we're going to be in each other's lives you should probably meet those most important to me right? Plus I was already heading out here and I wanted to see you so I said why not do both at the same time." He kissed her cheek.

"Hmph, ok." Sharonda said.

"What does that mean?" He asked.

"It means I'm still just trying to figure you out." She turned to face him.

"You don't have to try. I'll show and tell baby." Matt joked.

Sharonda laughed. "You are so corny."

"You like it though." Matt said.

Sharonda leaned forward to kiss Matt and he returned the gesture. "You're right I do." She said.

"I like you too." Matt said kissing Sharonda once more.

"Eww ya'll lame and corny. Come in here Ma and Dad about to finally tell us why they wanted us to come out here." Tierra said.

Matt and Sharonda laughed and walked inside.

"We just wanted to let you guys know before you leave tonight that we are going out of the country to renew our vows and of course you all are coming along with a few friends and family." Matt's mother said.

They all congratulated them and shared a toast to celebrating 40 years. Matt and Sharonda got ready to leave and shared hugs before leaving.

"Hey Sharonda, now we hope you're there." Matt's father said.

"Thank you. You guys' love is beautiful." Sharonda said getting into the car.

Chapter Seven - 3 Days 3 Hours

Dajon

The ladies toasted to a good time in California and living their best lives.

"Ayeeee it's lit!" Dajon said as she danced to the music.

"The concert is going to be even more crazy!" Marie said.

"Definitely." Sharonda said taking a selfie.

"Can we have some shots?" Dajon asked the waitress.

"Shots?" Marie asked.

"Oh you trying to go in?" Sharonda asked.

"You know it!" She downed the rest of her glass.

"Girl you sure about shots?" Marie asked giving her a look.

"Whats that about?" Sharonda asked.

"What?" Marie asked.

"That look." Sharonda said.

"Oh child nothing." Marie turned to Dajon.

"Yes! I'm good." Dajon smiled.

The ladies continued to enjoy themselves at the day pool

party.

"Excuse me ladies." A tall caramel skin, low haircut with waves, green eyed man said with his shirt off.

"Heeey." The ladies said in unison.

He smiled. "Ya'll good?" He asked.

"Yeah but we can always use more drinks." Dajon smiled.

"Ok ok. I'll send them right over but I came over here to talk to you." He said to Dajon.

Dajon followed him in the pool and they continued to talk. They were dancing when "Believe Dat" by LightSkin Keisha came on. Dajon started to twerk on him. He gripped her waist and started to grind on her as the song continued on.

He whispered in her ear, "you want to step out of the pool for a minute?"

Dajon nodded and followed him out until they were alone. They started to kiss and he went down on Dajon. She closed her eyes and remembered 3 days 3 hours before this moment.

Flash Back

"Ms. Le'aire, you may come on back." The nurse said.

Dajon stood with water in her eyes and took the long walk back to room 3.

"Remove all of your clothes, place them in this bag and put this gown on." She handed everything to Dajon.

Dajon took the bag and gown as tears left her eyes.

"Are you alone should I go and get someone?" The nurse asked.

"No I'm alone." She said.

"Ok. The doctor will be in soon." The nurse exited the room.

Dajon laid back on the bed and cried.

After the doctor completed the exam. She concluded Dajon was about 10 weeks pregnant. Afterwards she went home and took the abortion pill. For 3 days she cried and moaned and groaned.

Dajon called Derek, "D, where are you?" she asked.

"I'm busy baby what's up?" Derek asked.

"You were supposed to come over yesterday what happened?" Dajon asked.

"I got caught up and passed out babe." He said.

"I really need you babe. Can you come over please?" She asked.

"Don't start the clingy shit babe. I'm handling business girl." He said.

"Those hoes are more important than me!" Dajon snapped.

"Babe don't start that insecure shit man. I'm busy I'm working you know that." He said.

"Fuck you Derek!" Dajon ended the call.

Dajon balled up on the couch and cried. She wanted to call Sharonda and Marie but didn't want anyone to judge her so she figured she'd get through it alone.

End of Flashback

Dajon let out a few tears and pulled him up to her as they kissed he pulled out a condom and slid inside of her.

She kissed over his body and whispered "deeper."

He did as he was commanded and lifted her in the air as he went deeper and harder bouncing her up and down on his shaft. Dajon sucked her breast while moaning out in ecstasy.

They finished and gathered their clothes. "Yo what's your name?" He asked.

"You said you're visiting from Chicago right?" Dajon asked getting dressed.

"Yeah." He said finishing getting dressed.

"Well..." Dajon kissed his lips. "Remember LA." She walked out.

Dajon grabbed another drink downed it and returned to the ladies with shots.

"Ayeee ladies, shots!!" Dajon cheered.

"Where the hell were you?" Sharonda asked.

"Right." Marie agreed.

"Bitch I was being grown." Dajon said passing out shots.

"Bitccccccch!" Marie said.

"What happens in LA stays in LA." Dajon toasted them.

"Well aaaaaalright!" Sharonda downed her shot.

-Later that night

Sharonda stood in the mirror taking pictures.

"Girl you stay in that mirror." Dajon said.

"And do." Sharonda posed and they laughed.

Sharonda had on shorts, with a white body suit, and a hat with sandals. Dajon had on a romper with flats and her hair pinned up. Marie wore skinny jeans and a cute off the shoulders top and sandals.

"Ma'am, um you don't have on a bra." Dajon said.

"Somebody son." Marie smirked and pointed at her boobs.

"Yaaaaas sis! Somebody son about to get it." Sharonda said.

The ladies headed out to the elevator. The elevator stopped on the 19th floor to allow others onto the elevator. The doors opened and entered 3 men.

The ladies looked at each other as they all smelled and looked good. One had a low haircut with waves, another a fade, and another long hair stored in a man bun. They all had connecting beards.

"Hey ladies." They said.

"Hey ya'll." The ladies replied.

"Damn where ya'll from? Ya'll country as hell." The one with waves said.

They laughed. "We get that all the time." Dajon said.

"We're from Georgia." Sharonda said.

"Oh ok. My people!" The one with long hair said.

"You from Georgia?" Sharonda asked.

"Yeah I am. I'm Mason. This is Will (the one with waves) and this is Steve (the one with the fade)." He said.

"I'm Sharonda. This is Marie and..." Sharonda was interrupted by Dajon.

"Alisha." Dajon smiled.

Sharonda and Marie looked at each other and laughed.

"Alright nice to meet you ladies. Where ya'll headed?" Will asked.

"The staple center for the concert tonight." Marie said.

"Ok we're headed there too." Steve said as they all exited the elevator.

They walked out of the door and a car service was waiting for the ladies.

"Damn that's how ya'll rolling." Mason said.

"Yes." Sharonda said.

"Well we hope to see ya'll then." Mason smiled at Sharonda.

Marie

The concert was lit and the ladies were excited to have front row seats. As it neared an end a guard came out to Marie. She motioned for Sharonda and Dajon to follow her. They were invited backstage to meet Ty Dolla $, Chris Brown, Tory Lanez and featured artist.

"If Tory is single I'm not going back to the hotel." Sharonda said as they laughed.

The ladies drank champagne as they watched women come back to meet the artist.

Marie spotted Eric and smiled. Then she noticed a woman hanging on his arm. He hugged her and then she walked off.

"Did you see that?" Marie leaned over and asked Sharonda.

"Yes who was she?" Sharonda asked.

"I'ma find out." Marie said as she introduced herself and gave out business cards.

"Hey you're Marie Martin correct?" Trey Songz asked.

"Yeah I am." Marie was shocked. "How do you know me?"

"My stylist gave me a few of your pieces. I like your stuff its pretty dope." Trey said.

"Well thank you so much." Marie said smiling from ear to ear.

"If you have a chance I would love to sit down and talk with you about the grammys." He smiled.

"Yeah definitely. Here's my card." Marie smiled.

"I'll have my assistant set it up. Thanks so much beautiful." Trey hugged her as Eric walked over.

"Hey baby." Eric hugged Marie.

"Hi babe." Marie said.

"What's up E this you?" Trey said.

"Yeah man." Eric smiled.

"Alright I'm going to get out ya'll way my man." Trey dapped Eric.

"Hey ladies did ya'll enjoy the show?" Eric asked.

"We did thanks for asking." Sharonda smiled.

Dajon and Sharonda wondered off while Marie and Eric talked.

"So what's up baby? I missed you so much. I'm so glad to just touch you." Eric looked into Marie's eyes.

"I missed you too babe and I'm glad to see you as well." Marie said.

"What's up? What's on your mind?" Eric asked.

"Nothing. I'm good." Marie said.

"No I know something is wrong. What is it?" Eric asked.

Marie didn't say anything.

"Is it the chick you saw?" Eric asked.

"Who is she?" Marie asked.

"Baby she's a groupie that comes to every show trying to holler at Ty." He said.

"But she was on your arm." Marie said.

"Yeah because how else is she going to get to him?" He laughed.

"Don't laugh at me." Marie pouted.

"Stop that man. You're so spoiled. You know you my baby. I'm not checking for any other woman." He said pulling her onto his lap.

"It's not my fault. You did it to me." Marie smiled.

"There's my baby. As long as you're smiling I'm good." Eric kissed her cheek.

"Yo man I'm going to get up out of here." Ty Dolla $ said with 3 women on his arms.

"Aight man be careful." Eric said as they dapped each other.

"You ready to go baby?" Eric asked.

"Yep." She smiled.

Marie found Dajon and Sharonda. "Ok ladies. I'm going to get ready to go." She said.

"You leaving us?" Sharonda asked.

"Yeah she's going back to the hotel with me." Eric smiled and wrapped his hand around her waist.

"Aaaalright!" Sharonda said. "Somebody son." She laughed.

Marie laughed. "What does that mean?" Eric asked.

"Nothing babe." Marie said. "Bye ya'll."

"Bye." Dajon said.

"Be safe." Sharonda joked.

Marie and Eric finally made it back to the hotel. They exited the elevator and Erick covered her eyes. He opened the door and the room was lit with candles everywhere. On the bed he had a bag that read, "Chipotle."

"Babe you know I love Chipotle!" Marie jumped and hugged Eric.

He laughed and hugged her back.

Next to the Chipotle was a pink lingerie top and thong setting. Underneath that was a box with a necklace and earrings.

"Aww babe. I love it!" Marie said.

"And I love you." Eric sat next to her.

They kissed passionately until Marie's clothes were fully off. She got up and walked into the bathroom. She motioned for him to come and join her.

"Say no more." Eric said as he finished undressing and joined her.

Marie stood underneath the showerhead as Eric rubbed her shoulders and down her back. He reached around and squeezed her breast as he kissed her neck. Marie let out a soft moan. Eric continued to squeeze her breast and massage her body. He took two fingers and slid them inside of her until he reached her G spot. Marie through her head back on his chest and Eric massaged her G spot repeatedly.

"I'm about to cum!" Marie screamed.

Eric removed his fingers and allowed her to suck the juices off of his fingers.

"You like the taste?" He asked.

Marie nodded her head and smirked, "question is, do you?"

she asked.

Eric turned the shower off and carried Marie to the bed. "Let me show you how much I like it." He said.

He laid back on the bed and pulled Marie up to his face, "ride my tongue baby."

Marie did as she was told until her juices were flowing down his beard. "Told you I love it." Eric rubbed his beard.

Marie smiled, "I love you." She kissed him.

They continued to make love through the night together.

Sharonda

"Girl these niggas fine up in here." Sharonda said.

"Right and I'm about to catch one." Dajon said.

"Fishing pole, hook him sis." Sharonda laughed.

"And is." Dajon laughed.

Sharonda checked her phone and there were no messages.

"Girl who are you checking for?" Dajon asked.

"I haven't heard from Matt girl in like 3 days." Sharonda said.

"Well look F that nigga girl we're in LA at an after party with all types of celebs. Let's have fun!" Dajon said.

"You're right. Turn up!" Sharonda said as they walked to the dance floor and started dancing.

It was about 2 in the morning. "Oh my gosh bruh we're drunk." Sharonda said.

"No I'm not you're a lightweight I'm fine." Dajon said.

"Well let's get back to the hotel." Sharonda said.

"Ladies from the hotel!" Will screamed.

Sharonda squinted. "Who are you?" She asked.

"Girl stop screaming. They right here." Dajon screamed.

"Why you screaming?" Sharonda asked.

"I don't know." They laughed.

"Ya'll lit." Mason said.

"No we're not. We just had a few drinks." Sharonda said.

"Well we'll go back with ya'll to make sure you're safe." Mason said.

They shared a car ride back to the hotel and Mason suggested hanging out in the lobby with Sharonda.

"You good sis?" Dajon asked.

"Yes I'm good Dajon." Sharonda said.

"Dajon? I thought your name was Alisha." Will said.

"It is." Dajon said as they entered the elevator.

"Here's some coffee Sharonda." Mason said.

"Thank you but I'm good I promise." She smiled.

"You are really beautiful. I know your man misses you." Mason said.

"No he doesn't. I haven't heard from him in 3 days." Sharonda said.

"Wow I'd never go that long without talking to my lady." Mason said.

"Yeah that's definitely not normal. He usually hits me every single day since we started talking." Sharonda ranted.

"So are ya'll like in a committed relationship?" Mason asked.

"No. Yes.. We're just talking or shit I don't know." Sharonda shrugged her shoulders.

"Well if that's the case you should know you're worth more Sharonda and if that nigga can't see it, it's a real man out here that will see you just for who you are along with being as sexy as you are." Mason smiled.

"Aww you're so sweet. I know your girlfriend loves you." Sharonda said.

"She used to but we broke up about 6 months ago." Mason sipped his water.

"What happened?" Sharonda asked.

"She wanted to rush me down the isle and I'm not with that." He said.

"Well how long had ya'll been together?" She asked.

"4 years." He replied.

"4 years! Oh hell nawl. No wonder, that's a long time." Sharonda said.

"I mean how do you ever really know someone is the real deal?" Mason asked.

"If after 4 years you still don't know it's time to stop wasting each other's time." She said.

"That's true. I guess I was never really sure about her anyway." Mason said.

Sharonda nodded in agreement. "I'm actually horny as hell right now. So I'm going to head upstairs to my room before I jump your fine ass bones." She said.

Mason laughed. "Actually I wouldn't be mad at that at all but I'd rather you be sober first."

"That's true wouldn't want that drunken night type of shit. Been there done that." Sharonda said.

"And wrote the book on it." Mason agreed. "Before you go. What's your number?" he asked.

Sharonda gave him her number and went up to her room. A text came through on her phone and it read, "Did you make it to your room?"

"Yes I did thank you." She replied back.

She facetimed Matt. "Yo what's up gorgeous?" Matt answered.

"Why haven't I heard from you?" Sharonda asked.

"I'm sorry work just had me busy. Look at you looking all good." Matt smiled.

"Don't try to flash that smile I'm mad." Sharonda pouted.

"Why? What I do? You missed me?" Matt asked.

"Yes I did." Sharonda said.

"Aww you so sweet I'm sorry I really am." Matt said walking back into his room.

Sharonda thought she saw another woman's shoes in his background. "Are you alone?" she asked.

"Yes I am, why?" Matt sipped on his water bottle.

"Because I don't remember leaving a pair of heels at your place." She said.

"No one is here." Matt said.

Sharonda heard a female voice faintly in the background. "I know I've been drinking but I could've sworn I just heard a woman call your name." She said.

"Sharonda like you said you've been drinking. It's late I'm

going to go back to bed. Goodnight." Matt hung up.

"Did this nigga just try to play me?" Sharonda said out loud.

There was a knock on the door. "Who is it?" Sharonda asked.

"Mason." Mason said.

"What are you doing here?" Sharonda asked.

"Your girl is in my room with my boy. Can I hang out with you?" Mason laughed.

Sharonda laughed. "Sorry about that." she said.

Mason walked in. "So what's up Ms. Georgia. Ya'll just came out for the concert?"

"Yeah needed a quick little vacay. The same for ya'll?" Sharonda asked.

"Yeah its a vacation for my boys business for me. I'm a consultant." Mason said.

Sharonda and Mason continued to talk throughout the night. He was a good conversationalist, a businessman, a good dresser and he had a gorgeous smile, 6'3 and smelled amazing. He was family oriented and goal oriented. All of the qualities Sharonda liked and he helped keep her mind off of Matt.

"Wow this is crazy the Sun is coming up." Mason said opening the curtains.

"Wow we talked all night." Sharonda smiled.

"Yeah we did. Well let me get back up there I'll send your girl down." Mason joked.

"You got jokes." Sharonda playfully pushed him.

Mason hugged Sharonda and looked her in the eyes.

"What?" Sharonda asked.

Mason placed his finger underneath Sharonda's chin. At that moment Dajon stumbled into the room. "Girl hurry up our flight is going to take off soon." She rushed into the bathroom.

Sharonda looked at her and Dajon backed up. "You been in here all night?" Dajon asked.

Matt and Sharonda laughed. "Let me walk you out." Sharonda said as she pushed Dajon into the bathroom.

"Thanks for spending the night with me. You made it a lot better." Sharonda smiled.

"Any time. Have a safe trip back home." Mason smiled.

Sharonda smiled and went back into the room. She checked her phone, sent a few messages and began packing her bag.

Dajon showered while Sharonda caught her up on everything that happened.

"Aww that's sweet. My night was horrible and my stomach hurts." Dajon said exited the shower in a towel.

"It should all those drinks and then ya got ya some good D though didn't ya?" Sharonda joked.

"Girl it was trash. Total waste of my time." Dajon said.

"Damn." Sharonda laughed.

"Girl. I'm ready to get back home." Dajon finished getting dressed.

"I feel you on that. Are you ok though best?" Sharonda asked.

"Yeah." Dajon looked away.

"Best are you sure? You know you can talk to me about any-thing." Sharonda said.

"I'm good. Let's go." Dajon said heading out of the door.

Marie

Marie checked her phone as she finished breakfast.

Group text: Flight is leaving soon. Are you going to meet us at the airport?- Sharonda

Group text: Yes ma'am.- Marie

"Baby I'm going to hop in the shower." Eric said.

"Ok babe. I'm going to finish packing." Marie said.

Eric's phone pinged and then the phone started to ring. Marie ignored it until it pinged again. She glanced over at his phone. It started to ring again and the name was "Groupie LA."

"Oh hell no." Marie frowned. Knowing the password to his phone she unlocked it. She opened their messages and read them. She'd sent nudes to him and he'd sent a nude to her.

Marie gathered her things just as she heard the shower turn off. She walked to the bathroom door.

"Come here sexy give me a hug." Eric smiled.

"Who the fuck is this?" Marie held his phone up.

"You going through my shit now?" Eric asked.

"Answer the question Eric." Marie said.

"You went through my phone though Marie." He wrapped a towel around himself.

"This the same bitch I saw on your arm last night." Marie tried to remain calm.

"Baby..." Marie interrupted.

"Don't baby me Eric. So how long has this been going on?" She asked.

"Baby there's nothing going on." Eric walked toward Marie.

She walked to the bed and read the messages. "I miss you. I miss you too babe. Nude picture, dick pic. You showed all out for her. She gets the dick too?" Marie asked.

"No, she doesn't get anything babe. She's a fucking groupie." Eric followed Marie. "Baby calm down. I don't even want her." He said.

"Fuck you. Fuck her and you both can fuck each other." Marie dropped his phone in the toilet and flushed.

"Marie what the fuck!" Eric exclaimed.

She slapped him and left the room headed for the airport.

Chapter Eight-10 Seconds

Sharonda

A week had passed since the trip to LA. The ladies had been very busy and barely had time for conversation. No conversations had taken place about the trip seeing as when they returned everyone went back to their homes for much needed rest and recuperating. Sharonda invited the girls over for dinner and a girls' night to talk about the trip, have a few good laughs and catch up with regular life.

Group text: Still on for tonight?- Dajon

Group text: You know it boo.- Sharonda

Group text: I'll bring wine.- Marie

Group text: I'll bring more wine.- Dajon

Group text: Lol so I guess we'll have plenty of wine.- Sharonda

-Later that night

"So ya'll its been a whole week since LA. What's tea?!" Sharonda sat at the bar with her food and wine.

"Girl that trip was wild." Dajon said while eating.

"Girl you right it was. So let me tell ya'll what happened." Marie sipped her wine.

"What's up?" Sharonda asked.

"Ok so you remember the bitch that was on Eric's arm backstage right?" Marie asked.

"Yeah I saw that." Dajon said.

"Ok so he was like that was a groupie for Ty. So we get back to the room and of course I got some but the next morning we do it again and he goes to get in the shower." Marie said.

"Ok??" Sharonda asked.

"So I'm getting my stuff ready and packing up his phone constantly going off and I have his passcode so I look and it's the bitch from that night. Come to find out they've been texting and sending each other nudes and all." Marie said.

"Bitch whaaaaaaat?" Sharonda gasped.

"Wooooooooow!" Dajon exclaimed.

"So I show him and he's all you tripping I only want you and I love you. She's just a groupie shit and its not like that we not fucking." Marie ranted.

"Yes they are." Sharonda said.

"He lying like hell." Dajon said.

"So that's how a great trip ended. Shitty as hell." Marie lowered her tone indicating she was about to cry.

"Aww baby I'm sorry." Sharonda comforted Marie.

"Yeah he's not worth wasting any more of your energy." Dajon hugged Marie.

"I know but I still love him and it just hurts." Marie cried.

"Let it out boo it's ok." Sharonda said.

Marie went into the bathroom and got herself together. She came out with a roll of tissue. "I know I won't be the only one crying so here." She giggled.

They shared a laugh and Sharonda gave an out burst, "I been having sex with PJ." She covered her face.

"What?!" Marie looked shocked.

Dajon shook her head, "are you serious?" She asked.

"Its only sex. I needed my back blew out and so I did. But one time turned into 3 times and then that turned into sex on a regular basis." Sharonda finished eating.

"Whaaat?" Marie's mouth dropped.

Sharonda reached over and closed Marie's mouth and they laughed. "I know I know. But yeah that's my truth. Other than that LA was great and remember the guys from the elevator? I've been staying in touch with Mason we've been texting and facetiming each other." She said.

"Well I'll be damned. That's whats up girl." Marie said.

"Yeah and then there's Matt. You know I facetimed him while we were in LA. I'm not sure but I think there was another woman at his place. " Sharonda said.

"Bitccch what?" Marie asked.

"Yeah girl and then he rushed me off the phone. He was like I'm here alone but I think there was someone else there." Sharonda vented.

Dajon walked over after finishing her 3rd glass of wine. "Don't act like you ain't just say you been fucking that dumbass She said.

"Whoa you're in my face back up." Sharonda said.

"No like why you still fucking with this man? I told you about him bruh." Dajon said.

"The same reason you still fucking that cheating ass, abusive ass, fuck boy ass nigga you fuck with." Sharonda stood to her feet.

"At least it's a relationship." Dajon said.

"Oh that makes it better because you're ok with being cheated on? You're ok with being a side piece? Oh ok that's how it works I didn't get that memo." Sharonda replied.

"For your information he doesn't cheat on me anymore." Dajon crossed her arms.

"Oh yeah that's real cute after the 50/11 times he's cheated he's finally stopped. Kudos to your simple ass." Sharonda clapped.

"Don't judge me like your shit doesn't stink!" Dajon yelled.

"First off you've had too much to drink and you not about that life so calm your lil ass down in my house." Sharonda said.

Marie got up and stood between the two of them. "No fam she's pregnant." Marie said.

Sharonda almost choked, "what?" She asked.

"She's pregnant. Tell her Dajon." Marie said looking at her.

Dajon dropped to the floor in tears. "No I'm not pregnant anymore." She managed to get out.

"Anymore?" Sharonda still in shock asked.

"Yes I was pregnant. I didn't tell you because I knew you'd be pissed and go in on me." Dajon cried.

"So you told my cousin instead of me?" Sharonda asked.

"Don't make this about you right now fam. You see what she's going through." Marie comforted Dajon.

"Wow ya'll just fucking bestfriends now? You could've told me. I am always there for you no matter how dumb or stupid I think it is I'm always supporting you." Sharonda started to tear up.

"Well I'm not anymore. I took the pill for an abortion." Dajon cried. "It was so hard. It hurt and nothing could ease the pain. But knowing everything I've been through with him I couldn't take having a kid with him. So I killed my baby." She cried more.

Sharonda cried with her and hugged her. "Is that why you were wilding in LA and spazzing out?" She asked.

"Yeah that's exactly why. It hurts knowing I took my baby's life. It hurts knowing all I've ever wanted with that man is to have a family and he's had 2 kids with 2 different women while with me. It hurts my heart so much because I can't let him go!" Dajon screamed and cried.

Marie covered her mouth as she cried. Sharonda motioned for her to join them on the floor.

"Ya'll we have to be here for each other. We can't just go on with all of this building up. We have to let it out and lean on each other for support." Sharonda said as tears flowed down her face.

"You're right we do." Marie hugged her.

Dajon nodded her head, "I agree."

"And listen stop saying you killed your baby. You did not kill a baby. You killed what could have been but it was not formed or anything ok. You aren't the first and won't be the last to have an abortion. Don't beat yourself up over that bestie, ok sweetie?" Sharonda held her.

The rest of the night they encouraged each other and watched movies and drank wine until they were all asleep.

Sharonda got up to grabbed a shower to decompress. Once she was done she sent Matt a message.

Text: Hey listen, I went from meeting your family and hanging out with you nonstop to hearing from you only when I reach out or not at all. I don't get it but if you need to know how I feel I want to share it with you. Truth is I think you are an amazing man and I enjoy our time together. I look forward to your call or text or just seeing your face. I like that you motivate and are so encouraging to me. I want that in my life and most importantly I need that in my life. So if you feel the same way let me know.

Text: Hey Sharonda, of course what you said to me is beautiful. I think you are an amazing woman and I like hanging out with you too. The times we hang out and talk are some of the best times but I don't want to rush anything. I want to take time for us both to make sure this is something we want and allow God to guide us you know.

Text: I agree with allowing God to guide us and thank you for the compliments. You made me blush

Text: Then my mission is accomplished beautiful. You busy later? I want to take you to dinner.

Text: I can make time for you.

Dajon

The ladies said their goodbyes to one another and went on their seperate ways. Dajon thought about what Sharonda had said to her. She thought to herself, "why am I still dealing with this? Why can't I let him go? What about him makes me stay?" She got lost in her thoughts as the uber ride went on.

"Ma'am, excuse me ma'am?" The uber driver said.

"I'm sorry yes?" Dajon asked.

"We're here at your destination." He said.

"Thank you." Dajon said exiting the car.

Dajon saw Derek's car in her parking garage. "I'm not ready to go inside."

She grabbed her phone and made a call. "Hey if you're available let's link in about 15 mins." She said. "I'll see you then." She ended the call and headed out.

She freshened up in her car and changed clothes. She wore a cute plaid top with a black flare skirt and black boots.

She walked inside of Café La Cantina. "Hey I literally am about 15 mins from this place and never have I ever been here." She said.

Xaiver stood in a crispy white v neck shirt that hugged his muscles and 8 pack body and blue jeans. His dreads were up in a messy man bun. He smiled and hugged her tight.

"Hang out with me and you'll always get to experience something new." He said.

"Is that right?" Dajon sat down.

"Yeah it is. So Miss Dajon what prompted this?" Xaiver asked.

"What do you mean?" She smiled.

"You know what I mean." Xaiver smiled.

"Nothing, you told me to hit you when I was ready right?" She said.

"But the question is, are you really ready yet? Or I'm just something to do?" He said.

"Are you guys ready to order?" The waitress asked.

"Ladies first." Xaiver smiled.

They ordered their food and drinks and continued to talk. Dajon diverted from the subject and asked about Xaiver finishing his degree.

"Yeah so basically I just wanted to finish it so I can say that I completed it. I don't need it because my businesses are already very successful but to say that I obtained my degree and went back to finish it is big. Plus it'll make my momma smile." He laughed.

"Aww that's sweet." Dajon giggled.

"Yeah she always wanted me to finish so she'll definitely be at the graduation smiling ear to ear." He smiled.

"I will too that's big going back even though you don't have to. I'm proud of you." Dajon smiled.

"I love it when you smile at me." Xaiver smiled at Dajon and licked his lips.

Dajon blushed, "why?" she asked.

"Because it's so beautiful and I can watch you do that all day when you're really ready though." Xaiver sipped his drink.

"Ha, so we're back to that." Dajon chuckled.

"I'm just saying." Xaiver said.

"Ok so I didn't want to go home yet. I wanted to clear my mind and thought of someone that could help me do that." Dajon smiled.

"Now I feel like you're macking me." Xaiver laughed.

"I'm not, I'm being serious." Dajon laughed.

Xaiver smiled. "Well I'm glad I could help."

The date went on and they continued to talk. Xaiver paid the check and they left the restaurant.

"Where are we walking to because I have on these boots and I can't do too much walking all over the place." Dajon pointed at her shoes.

"Let me see." Xaiver stepped back and looked at her up and down. "I see you with the stiletto boots. Looking all sexy for me right?" He smiled.

Dajon laughed, "whatever boy. Where are we going?" she asked.

"We're here." Xaiver pointed.

It was a neighborhood garden with flowers planted everywhere.

"Wow this is beautiful but I don't want to mess up my shoes." Dajon said.

Xaiver laughed. "Such a woman. But nah really I stop by here every weekend just to check on Ms. Rose. She's the owner of this garden and I always bring her new flowers. This garden kept me out of trouble when I was a shorty. She would see me hanging out with the wrong group and would call me out to help plant flowers." Xaiver laughed. "But it worked because now I'm a successful businessman." He said.

"X!" Ms. Rose called out.

"Ms. Rose!" He called out.

He started to walk towards her and Dajon stood on the

concert. He walked back to her and picked her up. "Ahh!" Dajon screamed.

"Can't mess up the boots right?" Xaiver smiled and carried her over.

"Hey Ms. Rose." Xaiver smiled. "This is Dajon. Dajon this is Ms. Rose." He said.

"Hello nice to meet you honey." Ms. Rose laughed.

"Put me down so I can properly speak." Dajon laughed. "I'm so embarrassed. Hi nice to meet you Ms. Rose." She hugged her.

"It's perfectly fine honey. I can tell he likes you." Ms. Rose smiled.

Dajon smiled at Xaiver and back at Ms. Rose. "Thank you." She said.

Ms. Rose squeezed Xaiver's cheeks. "X I need some more lilies and some exotic flowers to put in this spot over here. Then I think I'll be good for now." She said.

"Yes ma'am I'll bring them by next weekend. That's all?" Xaiver asked.

"Yes that's all." Ms. Rose said. "Come here X look at this." She walked over to the side.

"What's going on?" Xaiver asked.

"You like her don't you?" Ms. Rose asked.

"Come on now you know me." Xaiver said.

"I do and don't rush this just wait on her." Ms. Rose.

"Yes ma'am I will this time." Xaiver kissed her cheek. "Here's some extra." He gave her a wad of money.

"Thank you X but you don't have to do this." Ms. Rose.

"I know Ms. Rose but I'm going to always be there for you. Until next weekend." He kissed her cheek and walked over to Dajon who was smiling ear to ear in admiration.

"What?" Xaiver asked.

"Huh? Oh nothing." Dajon said.

"Ready?" He asked.

"Yes. It was nice to meet you Ms. Rose." Dajon smiled.

"You too honey." Ms. Rose waved bye.

Xaiver carried Dajon to the side walk and began walking back to the restaurant.

"Wow I never met a guy like you before." Dajon said.

"What do you mean?" He asked.

"Just your ways its kind of refreshing to see." Dajon said.

"Oh I guess. I mean I was just raised that way. Take care of your people you know." Xaiver said.

"Yeah I get it." Dajon smiled.

"You been smiling a whole lot today. I wonder why?" Xaiver joked.

"I don't know why maybe I just like smiling." Dajon laughed.

"Well look thank you for calling me and I hope we can do this a lot more." Xaiver smiled.

"Yeah I have some things to sort out and yeah we will definitely." Dajon said getting her keys from the valet.

He walked her to the door and hugged her tight. "Do you always give hugs like that?" She asked.

"Like what?" Xaiver asked.

"All strong and safe. Comforting even." Dajon said.

"That's what you feel when I hug you?" Xaiver asked.

"Yes I do." Dajon said still holding her arms around his neck.

They leaned in and kissed each other. Dajon felt safe with him, it felt real with him, authentic and when they kissed it felt like Heaven. He wasn't trying to seduce her but just show how he felt in a sweet kiss.

"Alright Dajon call me and let me know you made it safe." Xaiver said closing her door as she climbed in.

"I will." Dajon nodded.

Dajon drove all the way home thinking of Xaiver and what it felt like to be with a real man all day long. He had his own businesses which were successful, he was a family man, goal oriented and educated. He was everything she wanted in a man but reality settled in when she pulled into the garage and saw Derek's car. She remembered her dilemma that she still loved a man who was abusive, hurtful, spiteful, and broke. He wasn't always like that so she had a little ounce of hope that he'd go back to the hard-working, sweet man he had been the first 2 years. Dajon excited her car and went to the elevator. She was caught in her thoughts when the door binged and opened. She walked down the long hall to her place and turned the key.

As she opened the door she heard the shower running. She opened the door and there was Derek in the shower with another woman.

Dajon went crazy. She began cursing them out. She beat him so bad that he ran out of her place naked. The chick was afraid to ask for her phone.

Dajon poured bleach on all things that belonged to him and her and threw it out of the window.

"Your shit is outside on the sidewalk. Take your dirty ass out there and get it. Sitting here in my fucking house you have to be out of your rabbit ass mind!"

"Baby I'm sorry. Let me back in please." Derek pleaded at the door.

"You begging that bitch wow." The chick said.

"Bitch I got your bitch!" Dajon opened the door with a bat. She started swinging not caring who got hit.

"I'ma fuck you up!" Dajon yanked her track out.

"You fucking with cheap weave having ass bitches!? You simple mother fucker!" Dajon yelled.

The chick ran off while Derek grabbed her and pulled her back inside as the neighbors began coming into the hall.

"Your clothes are outside. You have nothing in here. Get the fuck out!" Dajon screamed.

"Baby…" Derek began.

"GET THE FUCK OUT!!" Dajon screamed.

"I'm sorry." Derek pleaded.

"No you're sorry you got caught again. This time I'm really done. I hate you! I will never fuck with you again my nigga. I'm so good on you. Don't ever fucking say shit to me! I'm giving you 10 seconds to go!" Dajon screamed.

Derek left seeing how upset Dajon was he knew there was no calming her down.

Chapter Nine-Grave

Sharonda

Sharonda got dressed to go meet Matt for lunch and walked into the living room.

"Hey sis how are you feeling?" Sharonda asked.

"I'm sleepy I can't get up girl." Marie said.

"Well you're welcome to stay here. I'm going to run out and meet with Matt real quick." Sharonda said.

"In that!?" Marie asked.

"What's wrong with this?" Sharonda questioned.

"Girrrrl a maxi-dress? With no drawls!" Marie laughed.

Sharonda laughed. "I have on invisible line boy shorts thank you very much. And what's wrong with a maxi?" She asked.

"Chiiile you are something else." Marie laughed.

Sharonda's phone went off with a text message. It was a message from PJ with the 3 egg plant emojis. "The nerve of this nigga." Sharonda said.

"What?" Marie asked.

"PJ sent me the egg plant emoji girl." Sharonda said applying lip gloss.

"Girl I mean ya'll sleeping together that's what he want." Marie laid back down.

"I'm going to cut him off because of how I feel about Matt. He's so sweet and I mean I...really like him. I mean we've been talking for the past 6 months you know." Sharonda blushed.

"Aww look at you. I'm happy for you fam." Marie smiled.

"Ok well I'll be back. If you leave, lock up." Sharonda said.

"Ok bye." Marie said.

Sharonda headed out to lunch. She hopped in her car and called Matt. He did not answer and so she sent a text.

She pulled up to the rooftop and sat in her car waiting for him to show up. Her phone started to ring. It was a facetime.

"Hello." Sharonda answered.

"Hey beautiful. Damn who you looking sexy for?" Mason asked.

Sharonda laughed. "Can I look good for me?" She asked.

"Yeah that's all good. You look sexy though Ms. Georgia." Mason joked.

"Why you always calling me that?" Sharonda smiled.

"Because you so country girl, fine ass. So foreal though what are you up to?" He asked.

"Sitting in my car, remember I told you about ole dude, I'm supposed to be meeting him." Sharonda said.

"Oooh ok. I see. My bad you can call me later." Mason said.

"It's ok. He's late. Anyways what's up with you?" Sharonda turned her car off.

"That date I had last night was so horrible." Mason shook his head.

Sharonda laughed. "Damn."

"It ain't funny though." Mason smirked.

"Aww I'm sorry what happened?" Sharonda asked in between chuckles.

"Her breath was so bad and her make-up was caked on. It was just all bad man." Mason put his hand on his face.

Sharonda laughed. "That's crazy!" She laughed harder.

"Its really not that funny though." Mason chuckled.

"Aww poor baby." Sharonda laughed.

"Anyway you been waiting a long time sweetheart where is this man?" Mason asked.

"You're right let me call you back." Sharonda said.

"Alright. You deserve better Sharonda." Mason said.

"I'll call you back." She ended the call.

She looked at her phone, 55 minutes had passed by. "I been waiting a whole hour. He hasn't reached out or anything."

Text: Hey I've been waiting an entire hour. Where are you?

Text: I am so sorry Sharonda. I took a nap and overslept.

Sharonda read the text and left it on read. She headed back to the house and walked in.

"Girl why are you back so soon?" Marie asked.

"So I pull up this mofo isn't there. I end up waiting for a whole hour and he never shows. I text him and he's like he overslept. I didn't even text his ass back. Like really?" Sharonda sat on the couch.

"You think he's dating another chick?" Marie said.

"No he doesn't seem like the type. Maybe I'll just chump it up to men being stupid. They start to like a woman and back off per usual." Sharonda rolled her eyes.

"Or cheat. Fuck boy ass niggas." Marie shed tears.

"Aww baby. Want some ice cream?" Sharonda asked.

"No." Marie said wiping her eyes.

"You want some crab legs?" Sharonda smiled.

Marie nodded her head "yes" and both laughed. Sharonda grabbed her phone and placed an order through Postmates.

Meanwhile Marie's phone continued to go off with calls and messages from Eric. She ignored them all.

The food arrived and they ate and shared a bottle of Stella Rosa.

"Girl let me just throw this off in there ya'll be playing." Sharonda grabbed rum and poured some in her glass.

Marie was lit as they finished the bottle. "Girl shit where's my phone?"

"What's wrong?" Sharonda asked.

"I can't find my phone!" Marie said.

"Girl it's in your hand." Sharonda laughed.

Marie joined her as her phone rang. "Hello?" She answered.

"You finally answered." Eric said.

"What do you want?" Marie said a little tipsy.

"Have you been drinking?" Eric asked.

"That has nothing to do with what you want." Marie said.

"Where are you? I've been by your house and office." Eric said.

"Shit I need to go by the office." Marie said.

"Why?" Sharonda asked finishing her glass.

"I have that line shipping out tomorrow and Alex is reviewing it for me but I need to see it myself." Marie yelled.

"Why are you yelling I'm right here?" Sharonda said.

"Where are you? You can't drive I'll take you." Eric said.

"No! I'll take myself." Marie yelled.

"No I'll go with you. I'll call a ride." Sharonda grabbed her phone.

Sharonda called the ride and they headed downstairs as it was close by.

"Can we talk though?" Eric asked.

"No." Marie hung up her phone.

They got into the car and headed down to her office. Marie got out and reviewed the line.

"This is so important I had to make sure everything was perfect. You guys have done an amazing job." Marie said to her team. "Great things come in small packages!" She said.

"So look are you going to be ok?" Sharonda asked.

"Yes I'm good girl." Marie hugged Sharonda.

Sharonda called a car and headed downstairs. Erick approached Sharonda.

"Hey what's up Fam?" Eric said.

"Nigga. You got some nerve. What are you doing here?"

Sharonda asked.

"Listen I know you know what happened and yes it was fucked up but I'm trying to apologize and speak with your cousin. Please let me in." Eric pleaded.

"Your crafty ass! But my cousin needs a true apology because that was so fucking uncalled for. Fuck with my family again and watch what happen." Sharonda said with a serious evil look on her face.

"Shit ya'll definitely related. I know that look and I won't. So will you let me in just to go up and apologize?" He asked.

Sharonda moved aside so that he could walk in.

"Thank you. You good out here by yourself?" He asked.

"I'm perfect." Sharonda said waiting for her car to pull up.

The car finally showed up and Sharonda headed home. "Driver on second thought let me change the address." She changed the address where she was headed.

After about a 30-minute ride she arrived at a townhouse and rang the doorbell.

The door opened. "Come in." PJ said moving aside.

"Thank you." Sharonda walked inside.

"I'm shocked you're here." He followed her. "What's up?" He asked.

Sharonda kicked off her heels and sat on the back of the couch. "Does your offer still stand?" She smirked.

"You don't run shit here." PJ smiled.

"Shut up and come here." She said.

"Nah I sent that earlier. How you know I don't have anyone here?" He asked.

"Because I know you. Everyone is not invited to your house. It's a Saturday night and you're in the house." Sharonda said.

"Ok and I still could have had someone over." PJ said.

Sharonda chuckled. "Right ok I'll leave." She said.

"No hell nawl I'm just saying you don't run shit." He stood between her legs.

Sharonda wrapped her legs around him and they kissed. "I thought you wasn't trying to kiss me." He said.

"Shut up and stop trying to argue with me." Sharonda kissed him again.

They continued to kiss as he carried her upstairs. He ripped her panties off as they were almost at the top. "Nigga those were new!" Sharonda exclaimed.

PJ laughed. "I'm sure you have plenty from me anyway." He pushed his shorts and boxers down and slid inside of Sharonda.

"Ugh! You're so fucking cocky." She let out a moan as he hiked her in the air.

"You like it though." He said bouncing her up and down.

"I actually hate it." Sharonda said while moaning.

"Oh you do?" He began to bounce her harder and faster.

Sharonda continued to moan as she reached her peak. She climbed down and PJ placed her on the banister and went down on her in turn she climbed on top until they were both about to explode.

They looked at each other and laughed. "I can't stand you man you be playing." PJ said.

"I can't stand you either P." Sharonda wrapped herself in a towel.

She showered and came out fully clothed. "Well thank you sir." She said.

"Yeah no problem." He flexed his muscles.

"Whatever!" Sharonda giggled.

"No but foreal before you leave, you think we should try again?" He held her hands.

Sharonda was shocked. "Um, to be honest PJ what's a body without the soul?" She dropped his hands.

"What does that even mean?" He asked.

"We've been down this road before. We really do not work well together and can't stand each other. It's just sex and that has to go to the grave. So this is a goodbye for good thing. I hope for nothing but the best for you."

Sharonda leaned in to kiss his lips. "Bye babe."

Marie

Eric entered the building and went back to Marie's office. "Please don't kick me out just hear me out." He said.

Marie quickly sobered up as she crossed her arms and stood in place.

Eric stared at her.

"Speak nigga!" Marie yelled.

"Calm down baby." Eric reached for her.

"Speak from there." Marie moved out of his reach. "And don't tell me to calm down anymore. I am calm."

"She meant absolutely nothing to me. I fucked up. I know I did and I promised I would never treat a woman the way I wouldn't want my mother treated." He said.

"Well you failed there." Marie said.

"Listen I know I did and I apologize. Can you forgive me and just give me another chance?" Eric asked.

Marie felt herself about to cry. "I don't know." She said.

"I know I betrayed your trust and I know its asking a lot of you but I don't want you out of my life." Eric said.

"Eric I need to focus on myself for a minute. I almost messed up this opportunity because I was stressing over you. You fucking hurt me." Marie let out a tear.

"I know babe. I know and I'm sorry." Eric wiped her eyes.

"Just I can't have you in my space right now. I need a break. I need time." Marie stepped away.

"Marie we were building, we're just going to let that go for some hoe?" He said.

"A hoe you fucked! You did this. I need time." Marie opened her door and stood beside it.

Eric rubbed his head. "Baby why not just pray together?" He asked.

Marie shot him the most disturbing look. "No the fuck you didn't try to bring God in your bullshit. Give me time! Leave!" She screamed.

Her team looked. "Aye bro she said leave." One of them said.

Eric put his head down and headed down to his car.

The next morning Marie received a text message.

Text: Did you do this?- Eric

It was a picture of Eric's escalade with 3 flat tires and a key scratch from one side to the other.

Text: No. Maybe it was one of your groupie hoes. - Marie

Marie sent a text to the group message.

Text: Look what one of his lil groupies did ya'll. Lol.- Marie

Text: Lol that shit is dead!- Dajon

Text: To the grave with that! It was fun.- Sharonda

Text: Wait you guys did that?- Marie

Text: I plead the damn fifth!- Sharonda

Text: Lol. What else are day 1's for?- Dajon

Text: Holup what!?- Marie

Text: We love you! I'm going back to sleep.- Sharonda

After leaving PJ's house last night still on a high Sharonda linked up with Dajon and they both went over to Eric's house and showed Marie some love on his car.

Chapter Ten - Cut It Out

Marie laughed at her friends and went into the bathroom to get her day started. Her phone started to ring.

"Hello?" she answered.

"Hey Marie it's Trey." He said.

"Trey who?" Marie answered.

"Really?" He laughed.

"Trey Songz! Heeey!" Marie exclaimed.

"Listen I love what you put together. The looks for this show are dope." He said.

"Wow thank you!" Marie cheered.

"Ok so are you free in the next few months I have an international tour coming up and I want you there for every show." Trey said.

"I'm there definitely!" Marie said.

"Ok it starts next month. You can be ready in 30 days?" Trey asked.

"Definitely!" Marie said.

The call ended.

Dajon

Dajon and Xaiver have been dating since the day he took her to the garden. Classes have begun at the university. Dajon wrapped up one of her classes and headed to her office.

"Well hello Professor." Xaiver walked up behind her with flowers.

Dajon smiled and walked into her office. "Thank you honey," Dajon pecked his lips.

"You're welcome." Xaiver said as he sat down.

Dajon's coworker came to the door. "Well, well, well." She said.

"Professor Ann." Dajon said.

"Professor Mae." She followed.

The both of them laughed. "Ya'll cute or whatever."

"Babe you know Professor Head right?" Dajon asked.

"Yeah but I've never had to take her class, nice to meet you." Xaiver shook her hand.

"You too, have a good weekend girl." Professor Head said.

"You too." Dajon grabbed her things and locked the door.

Dajon and Xaiver walked to her car holding hands. "So what are we doing tonight?" Dajon asked.

"So we will be heading to a surprise." Xaiver opened her door. "Just pull up to this address and you'll see."

They drove to a spot downtown. When they entered the floor had a gold carpet with red roses all over. Champagne was given to them and music began.

"Aww baby this is nice." Dajon kissed Xaiver.

He walked her around until they came to painting canvas and a teacher to help them.

"Aww sip and paint babe! Thank you! You know I love this stuff." Dajon smiled ear to ear.

Sharonda

"What's up Sharonda?" Matt asked.

"Nothing much how have you been?" Sharonda asked.

"I've been good. Why do you ask like that?" Matt asked.

"Like what?" Sharonda asked.

"Like its been such a long time since we last talked." Matt said.

"Matt why are you wasting my time? We have barely spoken over the past few months." Sharonda said.

"Sharonda I am not wasting your time. I've just been busy trying to take care of the next stage of my life." Matt said.

"And you couldn't tell me that?" Sharonda asked.

"I could." Matt said.

"I've been only dealing with you these past few months and you know the feelings I've developed for you. I just feel like you are consumed and not taking me serious. I get being busy and all that because I have too but communication and consistency is all I've ever asked you for. You make time for who and what you want in your life." Sharonda said.

"I feel you. And I agree. I just needed some time. But I'm here now and I'm not getting out of your face until I get a proper hug, kiss and laugh out of you." He said standing in her face making faces.

Sharonda laughed. "You get on my nerves." She said.

"I know." Matt smiled.

They shared a hug and kiss on the pier.

"Matt, I have a serious question to ask." Sharonda said.

"Ok shoot." Matt answered.

"Are you seeing someone else?" Sharonda starred into Matt's eyes.

"What makes ask that? I'm right here with you." Matt replied.

"Because Matt you've been inconsistent lately and "busy" as you put it. We have gone from talking consistently and hanging out all the time to these fly by dates." Sharonda said.

"Listen Sharonda, I've been just figuring things out I promise that's it." Matt said.

"Are you sure? Don't lie. Just be honest with me Matt." She said.

"No I'm being honest." He place a kiss on her forehead. "Dang that phone been blowing up all day, your other man calling?" Matt asked.

"Oh don't do that. I know you not talking." Sharonda responded.

"Aight. I'm just playing. Give me a kiss." Matt said.

They kissed and Sharonda got in an uber. She was walking into the house as her phone started to ring.

"Hello." She answered.

"Dang Ms. Georgia. You finally answered." Mason said.

Sharonda laughed. "I'm sorry I was out and couldn't answer."

"Out on a date without me huh?" Mason asked.

"Don't start. How are you?" Sharonda asked.

"I'm good actually I was calling because I have a big deal coming up in NY and wanted to know if we could hang out?" Mason asked.

Sharonda was checking Facebook as they spoke and saw Matt tagged in pictures with another woman at his parents' wedding.

"What the fuck!?" She said.

"Huh? We can't hang out?" Mason said.

"Let me call you back." Sharonda said.

Sharonda screenshot the post and sent it to Marie and Dajon.

Marie immediately called. "Girl what's his ig?" She asked.

They started to research who the woman was and if they are dating. She had been tagging him in different post the past 2 months. This was the first time she had tagged him in pictures. They looked like they were on vacation and used to each other.

"Yo cuzz are you good? Marie asked.

"I'm pissed the fuck off. I was just with him and asked him to tell the truth. He gon say he been busy and figuring things out." Sharonda said.

"Wow. Are you serious?" Marie asked.

"Yeah girl fuck boy shit at its finest." Sharonda said.

Dajon called and Sharonda put her on 3-way. "Girl we need to roll up on that nigga?" Dajon asked.

"No. Yes...but no." Sharonda said.

"That's what they do though, real fuck boy types." Marie said.

"This shit hurt I cut everyone off for him." Sharonda said.

"Well what are you going to say to him?" Dajon asked.

"I don't know but I'ma call ya'll back." Sharonda said.

Sharonda hung up and cried then became angry. She called Matt to no avail.

"I'm so fucking stupid falling for a fraud." Sharonda said as she cried on her pillow.

Chapter Eleven-Girl

Sharonda

Weeks passed since everything happened with Matt and Sharonda. It was now time for the Christmas award celebration that Sharonda's job host every year. Dajon was there and Marie was there by Facetime.

Sharonda finished giving out awards and her manager, Howie, grabbed the mic. "Hello all, thanks for coming out to our very last Christmas award celebration. We will not be doing these anymore. So drink up and enjoy." Howie said.

Sharonda followed him to the side. "Why are we not doing these anymore?" she asked.

"Because I told you before you're putting too much into extra stuff. No one needs to be recognized for what they get paid to do." Howie said.

"You know what? Let me just say…" Sharonda was interrupted with announcement.

"Excuse me everyone thank you for coming. We want to acknowledge our amazing boss Sharonda Copely. She's supportive and always there for us. So this is an outstanding boss award! Thank you again Sharonda."

"Wow I am so shocked. Guys wow thank you so much. I have really enjoyed being here and working with each of you. This job has been so important to me but you know what I'm going to let you all know that these next 2 weeks will be my last. Thank you so much but I choose not to work in such a hostile environment. It has not been hostile until this last year with the hiring of someone new." Sharonda smiled and stared at Howie.

"So with that being said I wish nothing but the best for each of you and I thank you! Merry Christmas!" She walked away as many congratulated her.

Many of her constituents felt if Sharonda's leaving then they will too.

"Girl!! You just quit your job!" Dajon said as she hugged Sharonda.

"Yeah I know!" Sharonda laughed.

Dajon turned the camera to Sharonda. "Hey boo!" She said.

"Fam! I am so proud of you." Marie said.

"I know cousin." Sharonda wiped tears from her eyes.

"You'll be back before New Years right?" Sharonda asked.

"Yes! I will! Flight is leaving tomorrow." Marie said.

Sharonda and Dajon exited the party. "Sheesh it's late but we need food." Sharonda said.

"Boog's is open. Let's go." Dajon said.

"What the hell let's do it!" Sharonda said as they hopped into her car.

Sharonda and Dajon got to the lounge and were sitting in the swing chairs at the bar.

"Hey babe." Xaiver kissed Dajon.

"Whoa whoa whoa!" Sharonda nearly choked on her drink.

"Who is this?" Sharonda asked.

Dajon laughed. "X this is my bestfriend Sharonda. Sharonda this is X." she said.

"Well hello X. Interesting." Sharonda shook his hands.

Xaiver laughed. "Its nice to meet you best friend Sharonda." He said.

"It's not like that friend I promise. We've just started dating officially these last couple of months. He was one of my students." Dajon said.

"Dajon student? How old are you X?" Sharonda sipped her drink.

"I'm 33." He laughed.

"Oh okay then girl." Sharonda said. "Ya'll nasty, student and professor."

Dajon laughed. "No it wasn't like that. The semester ended and then he approached me."

"She played hard to get but man she's so worthy of me showing her how interested I was." X pecked Dajon's lips.

"Aww ya'll are so cute! I'm happy for you friend." Sharonda hugged Dajon.

Dajon and Xaiver headed to dance together. Sharonda video called Mason as it rang she had a tap on her shoulder.

Sharonda turned around and it was Matt. Sharonda hung up the call.

"Hey Sharonda." He hugged her.

"Hi Matt. What's up?" Sharonda pulled away from his hug.

"You look good as hell." Matt whispered into her ear over the music.

"Thank you." Sharonda sipped her drink.

"How have you been?" Matt asked.

"Good, great actually." Sharonda smirked.

"I see. We haven't talked in a long time." Matt said.

"You mean since I confused how I felt about you and you agreeing with me that you felt the same. Then seeing a social media post of your parents' wedding and some bitch with you after you just told me how you felt and we kissed, spent the fucking weekend together." Sharonda vented.

"It wasn't like that." Matt said.

"Well how was it Matt? I was supposed to go with you to the wedding anniversary. We kissed that very same day. I called you and text you and you wouldn't even answer the phone. You hurt me. You really hurt me Matt. I cut everyone off for you." Sharonda said.

"I didn't know how to say anything to you about that Sharonda. I had very strong feelings for you and then my ex came back into my life. I never meant to hurt you." Matt said.

"You are so full of shit! You were with her while with me, weren't you? Just admit it." Sharonda said.

"No I was not. I told you how I felt about you Sharonda. You meant everything." Matt said.

"Then why not just tell me you were interested in someone else? Why not tell me you weren't feeling me. You lead me on for months and then you made me feel like we had something real like it was leading up to something great.

We spoke all the time, we hung out all the time, you made me feel something I haven't felt in a long time and you played me." Sharonda teared up.

"No I didn't. I told you I wasn't with her I was only talking to you. We went to my parents' wedding together because she was there already on vacation. I only went there with my family." Matt said.

Sharonda laughed.

"I'm telling you the truth." Matt said.

Sharonda pulled out her phone and went to her cloud. "These are the screenshots I took of her tagging you on social media. Right around the time you started acting weird not really hitting me up anymore, returning my phone calls, or hanging out with me. She tagged you in all types of relationship post. Look at this one, "how you and I will be bae." Ain't that sweet. You went out with her family to hunt. Wow I didn't even know you like outdoor shit like that." Sharonda said.

Matt held his head down.

"No don't be quiet now love. Truth hurts doesn't it? Just admit you weren't man enough to tell me the truth. That's the voice I heard when I was in LA. Ya'll was kicking it for a while. My dumbass was just falling for you. Damn near love at first sight." Sharonda said.

"Sharonda I am truly sorry. I am so sorry I hurt you. You really meant a lot to me and your friendship does too." Matt.

Sharonda laughed. "Ha friendship. Lies you tell."

"I should have reached out. That's my ex and I wasn't completely over her. Its just the day I saw you I knew I wanted you apart of my life. I didn't mean for any of this to happen and for that I am truly sorry Sharonda. Can we be friends?" Matt asked.

"No we absolutely cannot. You don't understand the walls that I had built up you broke down. I cut niggas off for you. And out of all things, you know how I feel about meeting parents and you took me to meet your parents. Why? Why all of that and then not even just tell me the truth?" Sharonda asked.

"I am sorry. I don't know what else to say. I'm glad I saw you here. I wanted to speak and just apologize for how I handled the situation. I definitely had real feelings for you though it was nothing fake." Matt said.

"That's irrelevant now. You're in a relationship and those feelings I did have are done. I was happy being single and doing me, you could've left me alone. You chased me out of the Uber." Sharonda said.

"I'm sorry and I understand where you're coming from. I hope nothing but the best for you." Matt said.

"Thanks. Have a good life Matt." Sharonda turned to walk away.

Matt grabbed her hand. "Why you saying it like its goodbye?" He asked.

"Because it is goodbye. I don't have time for anything toxic in my life. You're apologizing but you came over here lying until I showed you proof." Sharonda said.

"I honestly don't know what else to say I just don't want you out of my life Sharonda." Matt pleaded.

"You should've thought about that before lying. I can respect your truth but a liar I can't deal with." Sharonda walked away.

Dajon

Dajon and Xaiver continued to dance together. "Babe I'm thirsty let me get another drink." Dajon said leading Xaiver to the bar. They sat down and toasted to new beginnings.

"Can you believe we're in this space right now?" Dajon sipped her drink.

"I definitely can I knew I wanted to be in this space with you when I walked into my very first day of class." Xaiver said.

"No you didn't." Dajon said.

"No it was the first time I saw you bend over in that tight skirt." Xaiver joked.

"Shut up." Dajon playfully hit his arm.

"No seriously though I did bae. I knew I wanted you to be my woman and give you all the love, support, peace, and everything else you've ever wanted." Xaiver sipped his drink.

"Aww babe you always say the right stuff." She stood in between his legs and wrapped her arms around his neck. I love you." Dajon kissed his lips.

Xaiver smiled. "I love you too."

It was the first time they'd ever told each other they love one another. They had been seeing each other since the day he took her to the garden.

Dajon hugged Xaiver and saw Sharonda arguing with Matt. Just then Sharonda walked back over to Dajon.

"What was that about?" Dajon asked.

"Just the typical fuck boy shit but I'm not going to let him ruin my excitement for the next stage of my life." Sharonda wiped tears from her eyes.

"Exactly Sharonda! I second that." Xaiver said.

"Hey we just met but I like him already." Sharonda laughed.

"Well good because he's a keeper." Dajon turned to kiss him.

"Listen the next stage you're referring to is beautiful and I want to do this before I lose it." Xaiver said.

"Listen, I told you I knew I wanted you to be mine when I first walked into class. I knew you were special and its only been a little while but I know what I want so if you want the same thing, will you marry me?" Xaiver smiled.

Dajon covered her mouth as tears flowed from her eyes. Everyone was staring and cheering on. Sharonda was standing in awe for her friend and grinning ear to ear.

"Say something to the man girl." Sharonda said.

Dajon looked back at Xaiver and ran to the bathroom.

"Let me talk to her." Sharonda went behind her.

"Girl what's going on?" Sharonda asked.

"What if I'm moving too fast? What if he's not the right one? What if he breaks my heart?" Dajon cried.

"Sweetie this is what you've been waiting for. This whole time you've been secretly dating him has he done anything to hurt you? Does he act like he's interested in anyone else? Have you met the important people in his life? What do they think? What do they say?" Sharonda handed her tissue.

"They are sweet and they love him. His mom and I surprisingly get along. We go to church every Sunday. He prays for me and he always makes sure I know how he feels or makes sure anything I need he's there." Dajon said.

"Then sweetie go and give that man a yes." Sharonda said.

"I'm scared bestie." Dajon cried.

"Aww sweetie I'm right here with you bestie. You know we ride or die. I got you. Most importantly God got you boo." Sharonda hugged Dajon.

Sharonda called Marie on Video so she could see the engagement unfold.

Dajon returned to Xaiver who was now standing and looking nervous. "If you still want to marry me, my answer is yes baby." Dajon smiled.

Xaiver picked her up and spun her around as they shared a passionate kiss. "You scared the hell out of me babe." Xaiver said in between kisses.

"I'm sorry." Dajon pecked his lips.

"Listen this isn't right away but I want you to know this is where we are headed and I'm very serious about you and us." Xaiver said.

"I love you X!" Dajon smiled.

"I love you!" X kissed her once more.

"Wait, oh my God! We haven't even met dude! Congrats baby!!!" Marie exclaimed.

"I know right but I'm so happy for her!" Sharonda cheered.

"Thank you ladies!!" Dajon smiled.

"Congrats Dajon." Matt said.

"Thank you." She said.

Matt stared at Sharonda who wouldn't look in his direction. He took a sip of his champagne and walked out.

Marie

"I'm so happy for you babe! Congratulations!" Marie said.

"Thank you Marie! Hurry back so you can celebrate with us!" Dajon said.

"Of course I will. I'll call you later fam I have to go." She said.

"Ok be safe love you cousin." Sharonda said.

"Love you too." Marie ended the call.

Marie was now in London, the very last show of the tour with Trey and Friends.

Trey was on stage and said to the crowd, "ya'll make some noise for my nigga Ty Dolla $ Let's do this shit my boy!"

They began performing as Marie stood on the side amazed that Ty was there, one of Sharonda's favorite music artist.

She backed away and headed to the break room as they finished their performance and entered the room.

"That shit was fire boy!" Trey said to Ty Dolla.

"Hell yeah! I'ma take some pics with the fans right quick." Ty dapped Trey.

After everyone left out Eric entered the room. "Hi Marie." He said.

"Hello." She continued eating.

He laughed. "You never want anyone disturbing you while you're eating." He recalled.

"Yet you're still talking to me." Marie said as she continued to eat.

"My bad. You look really nice and I see you're doing well.

You made it. I'm proud of you." Eric said getting food.

"Thank you." Marie said.

"I saw that you were a part of the fashion show yesterday." He said.

"You're spying on me, how'd you know that?" She asked.

"I saw you. Ty was there so of course I was there. I'm very happy that your dreams are coming to past. I just wish I was a part of it with you." Eric said.

"Thank you." Marie through her plate in the trash and started to walk out.

"Wait Marie, please don't go. Can we just talk?" He asked.

"About what? I don't have much to say." She crossed her arms.

"Well I have a lot to say. Its good to see you." He smiled.

"Don't do that. You follow me on social media and can see me any time." She said.

"Yeah but you know what I mean." He nudged her arms and smiled.

Marie rolled her eyes and let out a sigh.

"What?" Eric smiled.

"You know I love your smile." Marie said.

"I missed you." Eric said.

"Ok." Marie half smiled.

"Stop playing. You ain't miss me?" He asked.

"Ugh. Yes I missed you Eric." She said.

"Was that hard?" He smiled.

"Yes." Marie smiled.

"There's that smile. I missed you a lot. I know you're probably not trying to give me another chance but can we at least try being friends?" Eric asked.

"I don't know." Marie said. "Plus I need to go pack up so nice to see you." She headed for the door.

Eric followed behind her and turned her around and hugged her tight. It was the type of hug she loved from him. He smelled amazing and his brace felt familiar and comfortable. A wave of emotions rushed over her.

"Ok." Marie pulled away from his hug.

"It was good talking to you Marie." Eric said.

"Bye." Marie walked away.

After packing up her things Marie headed to the hotel. As she sat making sure everything was packed up in the room there was a knock at the door.

"Yes?" Marie opened the door.

Eric stood at the door with Marie's favorite cologne, Givenchy, jeans, a jacket and fresh waves and shiny beard.

Marie took a deep breath. "Hey, what are you doing here?" She asked.

"I saw you get off the elevator earlier and my room is down the hall. What are you about to do?" Eric asked.

"Just finished packing, flight is leaving first thing in the morning." Marie said.

"Oh I was about to go and have a drink do you want to have a drink with me?" Eric asked.

"No. I'm not drinking." Marie said.

"Isn't that a glass of champagne on the dresser right there?"

Eric laughed.

"Well I don't want to leave my room I'm tired." Marie laughed.

"Can I come in and talk? Please just for a minute." Eric smiled.

"Fine." Marie moved to the side and let him in.

Marie sat on the bed with her champagne.

"Dang I don't get offered a glass?" Eric asked.

"I'm sorry. Would you like a glass?" Marie asked.

"Yes I would thank you." Eric and Marie both laughed.

"You are doing the most." Marie handed him the glass and Eric took it out of her hand and grabbed her hand.

"What?" Marie asked.

"Come here." He pulled Marie towards him.

"Yes?" Marie asked.

"Listen, I know you're mad at me, I know you're hurt and over us but I miss you so much." Eric stared into her eyes.

"Eric come on we're talking right, doesn't that count?" Marie said.

"It does and I appreciate it but just be honest with me, you don't miss us?" Eric asked.

"Yes of course I do but I'm still hurt Eric. You cheated on me, you gave her what belonged to me and then you lied to me about who she was." Marie wiped her eyes.

"Marie, I fucked up. I really did and I know that but you were my rock. I think about you everyday still. I miss our conversations, praying with you, I miss my friend." Eric said.

"I get all of that Eric. I miss you too seeing you right now is hard for me. I want to hug you and kiss you and on the other hand I want to scream, cuss you out and punch you." Marie became emotional.

Eric embraced Marie and held her. "I'm not asking for too much Marie I'm just happy we're speaking. I don't want to rush you or put too much on you but I know my love for you hasn't gone anywhere babe." He said.

Marie cried in his arms and Eric continued to hold her while she cried. Marie screamed and punched his chest. Eric took it because he knew he was wrong.

"You feel better?" He asked.

Marie nodded her head, yes. Eric kissed her forehead.

"Thank you for not hitting my face though." Eric joked and Marie laughed.

"Don't make me laugh, I'm being serious." Marie said in a little baby tone.

"Aww my lil baby." Eric kissed her forehead once more.

Marie giggled, "thank you." She said looking up at Eric.

"Definitely no problem but as much as I am enjoying this moment I told you I wouldn't push so I'm going to go to my room." Eric said.

"Ok. I'll unblock you now and we can be friends back in the states." Marie said.

"I'll take that." Eric smiled.

He turned to head out the door and Marie stopped him. "What's up?" Eric asked.

"Hold me? I just missed being held and I don't want you to go yet." Marie said.

They climbed into bed together and Eric wrapped his arms around her. Marie looked into his eyes and they shared a kiss before closing their eyes and going to sleep.

Chapter Twelve- New Beginnings

Sharonda

The ladies were all at a lounge to bring in the new year together.

"Yo this last year was crazy ya'll." Sharonda said.

"That's right but it's ending on a high note!" Marie toasted her glass.

"OK! I see you boss!" Sharonda said.

"And me too!" Dajon toasted.

They all laughed. "It was rough but I think it turned out good for us ladies." Sharonda said.

"Better than good, Phenomenal!" Marie exclaimed.

"You know you're right girl. I finally got my Prince Charming." Dajon smiled.

"And girl he is a dream." Sharonda smiled.

"Ya'll I mean no lie he makes me smile, he takes my feelings into consideration, he loves to go out together, he gives me kisses and hugs just to say I love you, he will send me a random voice message and has all this excitement and it'll be like "hey babe! I hope your day is amazing mine is because I thought of you. I love you!" Dajon blushed.

"Aww that's so sweet." Marie smiled.

"I'm so happy for you pooh!" Sharonda wiped her tears.

"Yeah it feels really good." Dajon smiled and wiped her tears.

"And Marie you're an international fashionista now!" Sharonda cheered.

Marie smiled, "I am! Ayeeeee!" She twerked.

"Ayeee! I'll drink to that!" Dajon said.

"No but I'm super excited. While I was over there I met with a bunch of industry people and I have fashion shows in Paris, London and Germany coming up in the new year." Marie toasted.

"That's my mother fudging cousin!" Sharonda toasted. "More shots please!" she asked.

"I'm so excited ya'll like God is so good!" Marie cried.

"Amen!" Dajon agreed.

"Life is looking good." Sharonda said.

"You know what, I second that. And sis you took a leap of faith and quit your job. It's daring walking into the unknown but hey I believe in you! Everything is going to work out in your favor!" Marie toasted everyone.

"You got this sis. You're a boss for that shit and the way you did it. Boss shit!" Dajon cheered.

Sharonda laughed. "Thanks girl!" She exclaimed wiping her tears.

"Yeah cousin like listen you've been right there for us and I know God didn't bring you this far for nothing." Marie said.

Sharonda wiped her tears and sipped her drink. "Aww boo." Dajon and Marie hugged her.

"Alright so we have a few minutes for the new year to begin let's say what we're looking for in the new year." Marie said.

"I'm looking forward to happiness, beautiful love and planning a great wedding!" Dajon smiled.

"I'm expecting great things with my company, getting my degree, yep I'm going back to school! And I'm also looking forward to experiencing love again." Marie raised her glass.

"Ok I want stability, to run after my dreams, God, maybe love again one day and honestly living in the moment." Sharonda raised her glass.

"Cheers!" The ladies toasted.

"I agree to living in the moment." Mason smiled.

Sharonda turned around, "Hi Mason! You're in New York?" Sharonda asked.

"Yeah I told you I was coming but you were MIA on that part of the conversation." He joked.

"You talk so much shit." Sharonda laughed. "How'd you know I'd be here?" Sharonda asked.

"Them." Mason pointed towards Marie and Dajon.

"Ok girl we're going to give ya'll a minute." Marie walked away.

"Yeah I'm going to go find my baby." Dajon followed Marie.

"Uhh, ok." Sharonda smirked.

"You look beautiful." Mason said.

"Thank you Mason." Sharonda smiled.

"You're very welcome." Mason said.

"So what are you doing here?" Sharonda asked.

"Actually my deal went great and I'm here for good now. I have an office here in New York." Mason said.

"What?! That's so awesome! Sharonda hugged Mason. "Now I get to bug you whenever I want." Sharonda joked.

"It actually wouldn't bug me at all. I like you being in my life." Mason stared into Sharonda's eyes.

"Stop. Don't do all that big head." Sharonda sipped her drink.

"Do what? What I do?" Mason licked his lips.

"All that." Sharonda blushed.

"I don't know what "that" is." Mason smirked.

"Whatever so where's this office and where did you move?" Sharonda asked.

"Well let me pick you up tomorrow at 1 and I'll show you the office and then you can help me find a home because I have some places to go view." He placed his hand on her thigh.

Sharonda looked down at Mason's hand and back at him.

"What?" He asked. "Don't act like you not bae girl. You know you are." He placed his finger underneath Sharonda's chin and planted a sweet kiss upon her lips.

Marie

Marie was getting another glass of champagne and Eric walked up behind her. "Hey beautiful." He said.

"Hi Eric. I saw that you were working this party." She said.

"Yeah you know I always got to get the bag." Eric hugged her.

"Yeah I definitely get that." Marie said.

"I saw that you were here with your girls and wanted to say what's up." Eric said.

"Ok. What's up?" Marie replied.

"Nothing I see I'm still blocked I tried calling you." Eric said.

"I'm just confused E. I don't really know what I want." Marie said.

"I'm not rushing you babygirl I get it." He smiled.

Marie blushed. "Thank you."

"Yeah no problem." Eric said.

"Ok well let me get back to my girls." She said.

"Before you go..." Eric leaned in and passionately kissed her. "New year's kiss." He said.

Marie bit her lip and smiled. "That'll definitely get you un-blocked." She said as she walked away.

"Nah before you leave, right here, right now." Eric held her hand.

Marie pulled out her phone and unblocked him. "There its done." She smiled.

Eric kissed her again. "That's better." He smiled.

Marie walked back over to the bar where Sharonda and Mason were talking.

"Ya'll booed up yet?" Marie asked.

"Eww, don't do that. We're not you and Eric." Sharonda said.

"Oh you saw that?" Marie replied.

"And did. So don't do me." Sharonda said.

Dajon walked up with Xaiver and joined them. "Let the countdown begin ya'll."

They all counted, "5, 4, 3, 2, 1, Happy New Year!!!" Everyone cheered and hugged.

Marie found Eric in the crowd and winked. He smiled and winked back. "Happy New Year." She mouthed to him. Eric mouthed back "same to you" and smiled.

Sharonda

"This year has totally been wild and crazy but I'm ready to see what the New Year has in store for us all. Love, Happiness, Peace, Prosperity, and Growth to everyone! Let's ride the wave ya'll." Sharonda smiled.

They all shared a toast.

The next day Sharonda and Mason met at his office.

"This is really nice." Sharonda said.

"Nice? Girl look at this view." Mason pointed.

Sharonda laughed. "Whatever. I thought we were going to look for homes." She said.

"We are, let's go." Mason held the door open for Sharonda.

They went to view a few places but Mason wasn't satisfied just yet.

"Ok, this is the last one we have today. Take a look and tell me what you think." The realtor said.

"What do you think Sharonda?" Mason asked.

"I love it! This is the one." Sharonda said.

"I agree this one is great. Fireplace over there, view of the city, the guest bedroom is not near mine. Spacious, open floor plan. Most importantly big kitchen." Mason hopped on the kitchen island.

"Yeah I think it's great for you Mason." Sharonda smiled.

Mason laughed. "Don't do that."

"Do what?" Sharonda joined in his laughter.

"Look at me with that smile and those eyes." He said.

"Whatever. They're kind of a part of me." She said.

"Well while we have a moment alone, what do you think about that kiss the last night?" Mason asked.

"Um, I mean, I want to be open and honest with you. I'm still dealing with a lot you know and I just don't want to rush into anything and ruin it with you or anyone that could be great for me." Sharonda said.

"I appreciate your honesty and I get it. I understand we'll continue to build this friendship. In the mean time it's kind of cool to know you think I'm great for you." Mason hopped down and wrapped his arm around her.

"Is that what I said? I don't think that's what I said." She joked.

"Oh you two look great together." The realtor said.

"I know I'm working on it though." Mason smiled.

After signing the papers for the home Mason and Sharonda headed out to dinner. As they walked out of the building Matt was walking in with his girlfriend.

"Sharonda, hey." Matt said.

Sharonda ignored him and continued walking out with Mason. Matt continued to stare.

To be continued...

Chronicles of a Single Woman
Relationships, Friendships, Hustle

Made in the USA
Monee, IL
14 February 2021